CRAZY FOR YOU

Pink Bean Series - Book 8

HARPER BLISS

Copyright © 2018 by Harper Bliss
Cover picture © Depositphotos / photorista
Cover design by Caroline Manchoulas
Published by Ladylit Publishing – a division of Q.P.S. Projects Limited -
Hong Kong
ISBN-13 978-988-78014-3-6

To all the survivors.

Chapter One

JESSICA STOOD in front of the mirror with her eyes closed. She let her robe slip off and took a deep breath. She opened one eye to a slit through which she couldn't really see anything, then screwed it shut again. It was amazing how much of your own body you could avoid seeing if you applied yourself to it. But she had to look. It was time. Laurel would be there in fifteen minutes.

Jessica had seen the scars before, of course. She'd caught glimpses in the mirror. In an unguarded moment in the shower, she'd run a finger over their coarse texture—the red lines of remembrance. She'd never done that again.

Showering had never been a long dragged-out affair before, but now it had become an even more frenetic process. She disrobed with her back toward the mirror, hopped in, soaped up as quickly as she could, and only allowed herself to relax when hot water cascaded down her skin and she knew the ordeal of washing—of being confronted with her naked body—was over again.

Jessica sighed. She knew she couldn't avoid this forever. That was one of the main reasons she had made an appointment with Laurel. It would force her to confront what she was missing in a way she did not feel ready for at all. But she would never be ready if she didn't push herself out of her comfort zone. *Comfort zone.* Jessica hated the term. Her father had used it a few too many times when she was younger. But now she was using the exact term to get herself to do something she didn't want to do. It just went to show. In the end, she was a chip off the old block indeed.

"This. Is. Ridiculous," Jessica said to no one. Not even to her mirror image because her eyes were still closed.

She turned around, picked up her robe from the bathroom floor and pulled it safely around her shoulders. Only then did she open her eyes.

She couldn't do it. Yet. So what?

She took another deep breath. Should she cancel Laurel? It was probably too late. Canceling was always possible, of course, but she would have to pay the full amount if she canceled this late before the appointment. She knew the rules. In that case, Laurel might as well come over. If just to have a chat. She had no idea what had happened to Jessica. If she and Laurel only talked, Jessica could pretend nothing had changed.

Her body hidden away by the fabric of the robe, she looked into the mirror and examined her face. Strangely, little about her face had changed. Granted, her cheeks were a little hollower. Her eyes, at times, a little more sunken, but most of her features had remained the same. As if nothing had changed at all.

Jessica brushed her hair and forced a smile to her lips. She'd been lucky. One surgery and everything had been taken care of. It could all have been so much worse.

The smile remained without her having to strain to keep it. She'd have it ready for Laurel. How long had it been since she last saw her?

Jessica turned away from the mirror again and went into her bedroom. She'd taken clothes from her walk-in wardrobe earlier and laid them on the bed. The wardrobe had too many mirrors and she only went back in there once she was fully clothed.

She dressed and counted the weeks since Laurel had last come to her house. It had been so long that she lost count. Christ. It was time.

She headed down the stairs and waited. Outside, darkness had fallen. The clock read three minutes to nine. Laurel was never too late and never too early. Jessica knew the bell would ring at precisely nine o'clock.

She had opened a bottle of Cabernet earlier to let it breathe. Laurel liked red wine. Jessica didn't know why she wanted to please Laurel so much. She was the one paying her. Laurel was coming over with the sole purpose of pleasing Jessica. Yet she felt guilty for not having booked her for so long. For being out of touch. It was the craziest thing to feel bad about. No feelings had gotten hurt. Maybe that was what stung the most.

The bell rang as the big hand of the clock slid to nine.

Chapter Two

Jessica inhaled deeply and turned the doorknob. In a split second she would come face-to-face with Laurel's dark complexion, her surprisingly kind eyes—the warmth in them had always taken Jessica aback—and her easy demeanor. It was this particular quality of Laurel's that Jessica craved most right now. Since her surgery, it seemed that no one was willing to be easygoing around her anymore. As though acting normal would somehow break her even more than she'd already been broken.

Jessica opened the door wide.

"Good evening," the woman standing on her stoop said. A woman who was decidedly not Laurel.

"Who are you?" Jessica blurted out.

"Hi, Jessica." The woman held out her hand. "I'm Elizabeth, but do call me Liz."

"I was expecting someone else." Jessica ignored Liz's hand.

Liz nodded apologetically. "I know you were expecting Laurel. May I come in and explain?"

"No. I mean, not before I see, er, some sort of credentials. You could be anyone."

"I hate to say it, but I don't have my police badge on me." The woman produced a wide smile. She was nothing like Laurel with her soft curves and enchanting eyes. Liz was more angular. Taller. She looked somehow more unmanageable to Jessica. What the hell was going on here?

"Why didn't the agency tell me they were sending someone else?" Jessica asked.

"I'm desperate to explain," Liz said. "If you'll allow me." She tilted her head and painted on a dazzling smile.

"You can explain standing right there." Jessica crossed her arms in front of her chest, a gesture that still caused a strange sensation to run through her.

"Laurel has left the job," Liz said.

"What?" Jessica suddenly felt caught out. As though what she did with Laurel was all perfectly fine and legal as long as she did it only with Laurel.

"A few weeks ago," Liz said. "I've been taking over some of her clients." She took a step closer and leaned against the door frame.

Jessica instinctively stepped back. "That may very well be, but why was I not informed? You can't show up here and tell me this. I should have been notified in advance. I should have been—" Jessica swallowed the rest of her sentence. She didn't want to sound that crass. That's why transactions like this were not conducted verbally. It was all just too lewd to say out loud.

"I agree," Liz said. "Some wires got crossed at the agency. You weren't informed of the situation when you made the booking and they realized just a few minutes ago, when I texted to say I was on the way to you. I thought it better to explain in person."

"This is not the level of service I pay for," Jessica said. She really didn't want to have this conversation. She wanted Liz to leave. She certainly wasn't going to show her mutilated body to this stranger.

Liz nodded. "I completely understand." She narrowed her eyes. "But maybe we can talk about it? Work it out?"

"I wouldn't know what else to talk about with you." Jessica looked Liz in the eyes for the first time.

Her eyes were too light. Her brown irises had flecks of green in them. Her skin was too pale. Her smile too wide. She simply wasn't Laurel.

"I can think of a thing or two," Liz said. "Unless, of course, I'm completely not your cup of tea. There's no arguing over that." She crossed one ankle over the other and leaned against the doorframe, giving the impression she wasn't going anywhere soon. "But please allow me to say that I think you are one gorgeous woman, Jessica P."

"And you're obviously not very discreet." Jessica wanted to slam the door in Liz's face, but she couldn't do it. Her arms wouldn't move. Her body refused to go through the required motions.

"That's where you're very, very wrong." Liz's voice had dropped an octave. She looked around. "Let me ask you one last time. May I come in, please?"

Liz didn't have her profession written all over her, but Jessica didn't want her neighbors to start asking questions regardless.

"Fine." She dropped her arms and gestured for Liz to come in.

They walked into the living room and Jessica invited Liz to sit. Jessica picked a spot on the couch as far away from her as possible. She didn't want Liz to get any ideas into her head. As the thought ran through her mind, she realized it was one of the more ridiculous ones she'd had that night, which was quickly turning into an absurd farce. Things were definitely not going according to Jessica's plan.

It hadn't been easy for Jessica to send that message to the agency. But she had strongly believed that seeing Laurel would help her and had pressed *Send* after all. Only to end up in this situation. She would give whoever had been at the receiving end of her message a piece of her mind later after Liz had left. And call Katherine to tell her this was unacceptable. What did they think they were dealing in? The prices these women charged came with the expectation of absolute perfect management. But Jessica could hardly leave a bad review on Yelp.

She glanced at the bottle of wine. She could do with a drink right now and it would be too rude not to offer a glass to Liz, especially as two glasses stood waiting next to the bottle.

"Drink?" Jessica asked.

"I would love one," Liz said. Her teeth almost sparkled when she smiled, that was how white they were. "Thanks."

Jessica poured them both a glass then handed one to Liz.

"Cheers." Liz held up her glass. "To happy misunderstandings."

"What do you mean?" Jessica glared at her over the rim of her glass.

"Clearly a mistake was made and I understand you're shocked and unhappy about it. It's unprofessional and I'll make sure whoever is responsible for this cock-up never makes the same mistake again, but…" She paused to take a sip from her wine. "I, for one, am very happy to be here."

Because you get paid an exorbitant amount of money. Jessica didn't say that out loud. She couldn't say something like that out loud because she was completely complicit. And money mattered far less to her than the comfort Laurel brought her.

"What happened to Laurel?" she asked.

"She quit. It happens. This isn't a job you do until you reach the legal retirement age." Liz chuckled.

Jessica did admire her candor—and her sense of humor. Across from her sat a woman who displayed the same ease as Laurel had, perhaps even more.

"I suppose not," was all Jessica could say to that.

"This wine is divine," Liz said. "You have good taste."

"I don't need to be flattered or talked into anything—"

Liz held up her hands. "I know. Just to be clear, you won't be charged for tonight."

"That's not what I meant," Jessica said. She took a long swig of wine. However divine it might be, its exquisiteness was quite lost on Jessica tonight.

"It's all good." Liz picked up her glass again. "Any time you want me to leave, I'll go. Or, we could just chat for a bit. I have all the time in the world." She twirled the stem of the glass between her long fingers. "I'm a really good listener."

Strangely enough, Liz came across completely genuine. There wasn't anything fake or put-on in the way she sat there or the things she said. It was a gift, Jessica believed, to be able to talk to strangers as though you'd known them forever. Laurel had the same gift.

"Can I ask you a question?" Liz asked.

"Sure." Jessica took another big gulp.

"The first time you met Laurel… what was that like?"

Jessica scoffed. It was easy to see what Liz was trying to do. She could choose to rebuke her or she could play along. The latter would probably be most fun. Not having Laurel turn up had been a shock, but she was getting over that now. She was sitting on her couch drinking wine with an attractive woman who was, in fact, being very kind to her. Wasn't that what she was paying for in the first place? She could at the very least see where it would lead.

"Quite similar to meeting you." Jessica had a few very vivid memories of that first night with Laurel, but none were of the time not spent in the bedroom. "It's hard to pretend this isn't awkward."

"It doesn't have to be." That glittering smile again. "Anyway, I think it's time to move the topic of conversation away from Laurel. How was your day?"

Jessica broke out into a nervous chuckle. "Sorry, but that just seems too mundane a question."

"Would you like me to tell you about *my* day instead?" Liz pivoted in the couch and pulled one knee up, angling her body to Jessica. She wore a denim shirt of which the top three buttons were undone. Compared to how Laurel had always looked, Liz was quite casually dressed, even though on Liz a mere denim shirt somehow looked elegant. Her trousers were tight and black and glossy, not leather, but a soft-looking fabric nonetheless.

Truth be told, if Jessica had passed Liz in the street, she would have stopped to look twice.

"Sure. Do tell." Jessica drank again and allowed the alcohol to relax her.

"Let's see." Liz fixed her gaze on Jessica's, as though she was about to tell her the sexiest story instead of a recap of her day. Or perhaps her day had been sexy. "I woke up late. Went for a run in Centennial Park. Had lunch—smashed avocado on toast, for your information." She paused. "In the afternoon I went to a TRX class." She flexed her arm and pretended to feel her biceps. "Got to keep these babies toned." The grin she shot Jessica next was goofy rather than seductive. "Then I read the newspaper, wasted some time on the internet, took a long bath, had a disco nap followed by a light dinner, and now I'm here." She arched up her eyebrows. "Pretty mundane indeed."

"A run *and* a TRX class?" The mere thought of it

exhausted Jessica, even though she wasn't quite sure what TRX stood for. Physical conditioning was next on her 'to do list'—but first she wanted to work on her self-respect a little more. "You must be very tired."

Liz shook her head. "On the contrary."

Jessica imagined Liz running in the park. Her shoulders were broad, filling out her shirt in the most magnificent way. She pictured Liz in a tank top, a sheen of sweat glistening on her skin. The image ignited a light tingle in her lower belly. She was glad to discover that her most neglected organ still showed signs of being alive.

"It gives me energy and, well, my body is my biggest asset," Liz said matter-of-factly.

Jessica nearly sputtered out the sip of wine she'd just drunk. One thing was for sure, Liz had no qualms about being open about the job she did.

"Is it really, though?" Jessica asked. She hadn't meant to ask the question, hadn't thought about it, she'd just blurted it out. It was the closest she'd come to a real conversation with Liz since she had turned up.

"How do you mean?" Liz lightly ran a fingertip over her knee.

The motion distracted Jessica. She was pretty sure her meaning was clear to Liz, but Jessica didn't mind answering the question. So Liz wanted her to say certain things. Now that she had a bit of wine in her, and was getting used to the not unpleasant sight of Liz, that was fine. "Of course, I can see how your body is important, but I dare to guess other skills are equally, if not more, important."

"Which skills might they be?"

Jessica chuckled. "Do you really want me to have a go at trying to sum up your social skills?"

Liz shook her head. "Absolutely not." She grinned at Jessica. "Now would you like to tell me about *your* day?"

Jessica sighed. "There's really not much to tell. I mainly watched a lot of Netflix, but don't even ask me which shows. I was just passing time more than paying attention."

Liz narrowed her eyes. "Not what I expected. You don't strike me as the kind of woman who sits around and does nothing all day."

Jessica didn't reply immediately. Then she mumbled, "I'm still convalescing, I guess."

"Sorry? I didn't quite get that." Liz shuffled a little closer.

"I had surgery a while ago. I haven't gone back to work yet. Going back next week, though." Jessica forced her voice to be louder, making it sound unnatural.

"How do you feel about that?" Liz asked.

What was this? Rent-a-shrink? Jessica shrugged. She didn't have strong feelings about anything lately. As though something inside of her had gone numb when they'd taken a scalpel to her body and removed a body part she could live without.

"I'm sure it'll beat watching Netflix all day," she said laconically.

"Are you in pain?" Liz asked. "After your surgery?"

"Not anymore," Jessica lied, because sometimes she felt the most acute pain in the very part of her body that wasn't there anymore. A pain she could do nothing about because it was all in her head—where else could it possibly be?

Liz glanced at her and sent her a soft smile. She put her glass down, held up her hands, and wiggled her fingers. "I give a mean massage," she said. "As hard or soft as you like."

Jessica didn't know what to say to that so she just stared at Liz's hands—and her long, strong fingers. It was decision time again. "That's very nice of you to offer, but I'm good."

"Let me know if you change your mind." Liz drummed her fingertips on her thigh. "You look a bit tense around the shoulders."

Jessica huffed out some pent-up air.

"I'm sorry. I didn't quite catch that either," Liz said, a wide smile on her face again.

"I was trying to picture how I'm coming across. Obviously, you know who I am. You did your research. I'm sure the agency has a file on me. Part of me would like to know whether Laurel shared certain details about me, although the other part of me prefers not to think about that. I can only imagine this evening is not going according to your plan at all. And that you hadn't counted on meeting such an uptight rich girl, having to slog through this awkward conversation with me."

"That's not how I think of you at all, Jessica." Liz's voice had gone all soft and buttery. "And just to put your mind at ease, no details are shared between us at the agency. Discretion is the key to our success. There are no files, although I have, of course, looked you up online." She sank her teeth into her bottom lip for a split second. "Can't say I found much. Discretion seems to be very important to you as well."

"It should be to more people." Jessica didn't feel like divulging the real reason for the meagre results a Google search of her name yielded.

"That's so very true." Liz smiled again. "All of that being said, and since we were talking about my possible other skills earlier…" She looked Jessica in the eye again. "I can clearly sense you're feeling ill at ease. Not so much about me, although having me turn up when you were expecting Laurel has understandably thrown you. You don't seem to be very comfortable in your skin. Perhaps the surgery you talked about earlier has something to do with that?"

Jessica hadn't seen her therapist since before the surgery. She was beginning to think that was a mistake. Liz was playing shrink with her and it was having an unmistakable effect on her—the jury was still out on whether it was a positive or negative effect, but Jessica was just glad to be feeling something other than the dread she faced when looking into the mirror.

"You know what, Liz?" She smiled back. "I think I might be up for a bit of a shoulder massage."

Chapter Three

"It would be my pleasure." Liz rose and looked around the room. "Why don't you sit in that chair over there." She pointed at the low-backed armchair in which Jessica liked to curl up with a book—even though she hadn't read more than the odd page lately. "Put your feet up." Liz dragged the ottoman close. "I'll do the rest."

Jessica followed her instructions. By the time she sat, her shoulders were so tense, she couldn't wait for Liz's fingers to dig in.

"I'm just going to massage you over your blouse. Is that okay?" Liz asked, her voice a soft whisper.

"Yes." Jessica concluded that one of Liz's other skills was a sixth sense as to which items of clothing her clients were comfortable removing at any given time. Jessica was nowhere near ready to lower her blouse, let alone take it off in front of a stranger. Although, when she was clothed, if you didn't know about her surgery, and didn't look too closely, you probably couldn't tell.

Liz ran her fingers over the back of Jessica's head, then the base of her skull, as though she was trying to get a feel and read the level of tension residing in that area of Jessica's body.

Her fingertips caressed the exposed skin above the collar of her blouse. They dipped in a fraction, stroking her neck, before moving to her shoulders, over the fabric of Jessica's blouse.

Jessica was glad she was wearing a long-sleeved blouse because her skin broke out into goose bumps. She hadn't been touched like this in so long. With tenderness, as opposed to the directness of a nurse's skilled hands when she changed Jessica's bandages.

Over Jessica's blouse, Liz circled her thumbs next to Jessica's shoulder blades, the very spot where Jessica always suffered from various stress-related aches. When Liz's thumbs sunk in, Jessica couldn't suppress a gasp of pure pleasure.

Liz reacted by applying more pressure and gradually expanding the area she was working on. She dug her fingers into the hard-knotted muscles of Jessica's shoulders, pressed her knuckles against the most persistent knots, and worked magic with her thumbs until Jessica felt a wave of tension just flow out of her, as though Liz was absorbing it through her fingertips.

Jessica had lost track of time and had no idea how long Liz had been massaging her shoulders, but she hadn't strayed beyond the boundaries of her blouse. The motion of Liz's hands slowed and then Jessica felt Liz's breath near her ear.

"Would you like me to do your neck as well?" she whispered, making it sound like a very sexy proposition.

"Yes, please." Jessica barely recognized her own voice.

"Okay," Liz said. "Just relax." She started by pushing the collar of Jessica's blouse down a little. Jessica responded by undoing one button so she could expose a little more skin on her neck.

"I'll just be a second," Liz said.

Jessica watched Liz go over to the couch and pick up her bag, which she'd left next to it. When Liz returned to her position behind her, Jessica heard her rustling through the bag. She heard more rustling, followed by a squirting noise, and the sound of hands being rubbed together with some lotion or oil between them.

Liz's hands were slick and warm when they touched down on Jessica's neck.

Innocent though it seemed, Jessica hadn't been touched this intimately since she'd shared a bed with three other women, one of whom she'd paid for her services.

So many thoughts ran through her head. When would she be able to share intimacy with someone she loved again? She had a long way to go before that could happen. First, she'd have to be able to show herself—*to* herself. That was the first step. Perhaps this evening wasn't going as planned, but it was helping. The sensation of Liz's skilled fingers kneading her neck, running up and down the sensitive skin along the side of it, was taking down a little more of her guard with every tiny motion.

For a brief moment, Jessica considered asking for a full back massage, that was how divine Liz's hands felt on her flesh. But she didn't. The words didn't come out of her mouth and she knew that was because she wasn't ready to speak them—she wasn't ready for anything other than her blouse collar being pushed down a fraction.

"That was divine," Jessica said when the neck massage was over.

"I'm glad." Liz's hands hadn't ventured any lower than Jessica had felt comfortable with. She hadn't pushed Jessica's boundaries in any way. Maybe she sensed that Jessica wasn't ready. Maybe her sixth sense was her superpower. "Can I wash my hands somewhere?"

Jessica pointed Liz to the bathroom in the hallway and

took the moment alone to regroup. What would happen next? It was entirely up to her. She could ask Liz to leave. She would never have to see her again. Or she could pour her another glass of wine and they could continue their chat. Jessica might not be ready for a number of things just yet, but she was up to having a more candid conversation. Maybe if she just spoke the words to someone new, if they were out there in the atmosphere, it would be easier to open her eyes next time she stood in front of the mirror.

Liz's hair fell into her eyes and she brushed it aside with an exquisite hand gesture as she returned and headed toward the couch.

"Would you like another glass of wine?" Jessica asked.

"I would love one." Liz sat on the corner of the couch closest to Jessica's armchair.

Jessica started to rise, but Liz held up her hand. "Let me," she said. "You just relax a little more."

Jessica watched her hop out of the couch with elegant swiftness. She wondered how old Liz was. Come to think of it, she'd never known Laurel's age. She'd seen every nook and cranny of her body, and she had hazarded many a guess, but Laurel had never confirmed nor denied a number she offered.

Liz topped up their glasses and when she handed Jessica hers, she sent her a small smile. It was the kind of subtle smile that made Jessica imagine all sorts of things. Things she could have happen at the drop of a hat if she wanted them to. That was why Liz had come here in the first place.

"Thanks," Jessica said and held Liz's gaze. What had she had against the color of her eyes earlier? That they were lighter than Laurel's? How silly. Just like Laurel, Liz had beautiful eyes.

Once Liz had sat again, her body leaning against the armrest of the couch, Jessica said, "I had a mastectomy.

Breast cancer. I guess I was lucky that only my right breast had to be removed." Her shoulders hunched, as though she was trying to obscure her chest from view.

"I'm so sorry. That must have been hard." Liz didn't sound very surprised.

"It was hard, but I also got lucky. I got to keep one." Jessica had to stop herself from putting a protective hand on her left breast. "The biggest one." She managed a chuckle.

"You haven't had reconstructive surgery?" Liz asked, a warm smile forming on her lips.

"I was advised to wait at least half a year, in case I still needed radiation after the surgery. But I got lucky again. No radiation necessary. So far."

"That's good." Liz looked into her wine glass, then up again. "You are lucky, even though getting cancer might not make you feel so lucky."

Jessica drank before she spoke again. "It could have been a lot worse. I understand this very well." She sighed. "I've been made very aware of my… mortality, I guess. Along with some other issues."

Liz looked at her but didn't say anything. In her profession, being a good listener was probably as important as keeping a fit body.

"I suddenly found myself at the age of forty-five without many people I could call genuine friends, without a family that cared beyond getting me the fanciest room in a private clinic, without a significant other, and without my right breast." Jessica was aware of how pathetic she sounded. She squared her shoulders, making sure not to push her chest forward as she did, and looked Liz in the eye. An honest analysis of her life didn't automatically make her pathetic. It was just how things were—and she wasn't after Liz's pity.

"That mustn't be easy for someone who most people think has it all."

Jessica waved off Liz's comment. "I stopped caring about what others think of me a while back." She painted on a wide grin. "And at least I have money. No matter how badly I fuck up, I will always have money. As crass as it may sound, there's some comfort in that."

"I don't think there's anything crass about money." Liz mirrored her grin. "That would be quite hypocritical, doing what I do."

Jessica narrowed her eyes. "Is this your only job?"

Liz nodded. "And a well-paid one at that."

"Don't I know it." Jessica actually chuckled.

"But everything's free tonight." Liz leaned over the armrest a bit more. "Are you sure you don't want another massage? Take advantage of the situation?"

"I'm not after a freebie." Jessica shook her head. An idea popped into her head. "But since you're still here, I'd like to ask you for another favor, if you don't mind."

"Anything except plumbing," Liz joked. "I'm really no good at that."

"I haven't been out all day." Jessica scrunched her lips together. "In fact, I haven't been out since my last visit to the hospital three days ago. Will you come with me for a walk around the neighborhood?"

"It would be my pleasure." Liz jumped up energetically. "It's a lovely spring evening."

"Great." Jessica rose from her seat with considerably less energy.

Chapter Four

WHEN THEY'D STOOD outside Jessica's door, Liz had offered her arm for Jessica to hook hers through, and she had happily taken the opportunity. Walking around this Sydney neighborhood, to which she'd only moved a year ago, and under the current circumstances in which she often felt too fragile for the outside world, was so much easier on the arm of this gorgeous woman.

They walked in silence along MacLeay Street, meandering into smaller side streets. A few pubs had put out tables and chairs on the sidewalk already, but it was still a little too chilly to sit outside.

"Good thing I'm a sensible shoe girl," Liz said after a while.

"*There*'s a phrase that could be taken in more ways than one," Jessica replied. She steered them around. They'd walked for twenty minutes and still had to make it back to her house. She was getting tired.

Liz laughed heartily. She held on to Jessica's arm a little tighter. "I know you're going through a hard time right now and you're probably not yourself entirely, but I get the impression that sometimes glimpses of your old self come through. I like it."

"Ah, my old self." Jessica breathed in a fresh gulp of evening air. "If I focus really hard, I sometimes remember her."

"That sounded very dramatic." Liz lightly bumped into Jessica.

"Drama might very well be the Porter family specialty. Or better, how to be inundated by it while all you try to do is avoid it."

They both chuckled and it felt so good to have a little giggle with another woman by her side. Until Jessica remembered that she was paying for the experience—there was no way she would accept not paying after all the time Liz had spent with her. It wasn't her fault that Jessica had no idea she would show up. And now that they were walking along the dark streets of Pott's Point, she'd all but forgotten about Laurel.

"Is this what they call *The Girlfriend Experience*?" Jessica asked.

A deep laugh bubbled from Liz's throat. "Not quite."

"Is that something you get asked to do often?" Jessica had never dared ask Laurel questions like that. The vibe between them hadn't really invited them. Tonight, however, she was experiencing intimacy—paid for, but intimacy nonetheless—of a different kind.

"I'd rather not talk about that." Liz turned to face Jessica and painted on a wide smile—probably to make her rebuttal of Jessica's question go down a little easier.

"Fair enough," Jessica said.

"Ask me anything else instead," Liz said.

Their footfalls could barely be heard on the sidewalk.

Jessica had worn comfortable shoes as well. She was going for a walk, not attending an ANBC board meeting. Although she wished she'd worn heels so Liz didn't dwarf her so much.

"Anything?" Jessica asked. "Are you sure?"

"Anything," Liz confirmed.

"How long have you been in this job?" Jessica had a number of pressing questions battling for the upper hand in her brain, but this was the one she chose to ask.

"A few years," Liz said.

"That's pretty vague. Kind of makes me feel I wasted my question." They were approaching the dead-end street Jessica lived on.

"Ask me another one then. And make sure I can't give you a vague answer." There was obvious glee in Liz's voice.

Jessica tried to sort through her thoughts. In the end, she found herself only capable of asking one very specific question. "Will you come back some day and finish that massage?" The question surprised her as well. Of all the things she could have asked she asked a question she could have gotten the answer to just by making a request to the agency. But she wanted to hear the words come from Liz's mouth.

"I would love to." Liz held on to Jessica's arm a little tighter. They turned into Jessica's street and, although she was slightly out of breath and getting more tired with every second that passed, Jessica suddenly found herself regretting that their walk was about to end. "Any time," Liz said.

"Will you make sure they don't send someone else?" Jessica asked as they halted in front of her house.

"I give you my word." Liz let her hand slide from Jessica's arm to her hand and slipped her fingers through Jessica's.

Jessica couldn't think of a better example of what she thought of as *the girlfriend experience*, but instead of ruining the moment by describing it, she decided to enjoy the touch of this beautiful woman's fingers sliding against her own.

"Will you come in for a brief moment?" Jessica asked.

Liz nodded.

Jessica unlocked the door and they stood in the hallway. Because Jessica had expected Laurel, she had put the agreed-upon sum in an envelope and put it in a drawer in the hallway cabinet, that way she could pay Laurel as she let her out—and the exchange of money could be relegated to a brief afterthought.

Jessica opened the drawer and retrieved the envelope she had prepared. She gave it to Liz. "Please. No arguments."

Liz regarded the envelope. How many of these did she hold in her hands every week? Jessica had so many questions popping into her head again. Questions she was always so easily able to push to the back of her mind when she was with Laurel. Probably because the transaction with Laurel had always been very different—much more to the point.

"I want to protest," Liz said. "But I also don't want you to feel bad about not paying me. In the end, it's your call."

"Take the money," Jessica said. "The time you spent with me was worth far more than what's in that envelope."

"Thank you." Liz smiled, a glint of overhead light catching in her eyes. "I appreciate that." She leaned forward and kissed Jessica on the cheek. "I can stay longer if you want me to."

"I'm really tired. Too much excitement for one day." It wasn't even a quip. Who knew feeling alive for a few brief moments could take up so much energy?

"I understand." Liz touched her hand lightly against Jessica's shoulder. "I hope to see you again soon." She opened her arms wide and drew Jessica in for a hug.

"Me too," Jessica mumbled against Liz's shoulder.

After Liz had left, Jessica stood staring at the door for a while longer, leaning against the cabinet out of which she had taken the envelope of money. Jessica couldn't quite get her head around what had happened tonight. It hadn't come close to anything she had expected.

Chapter Five

"I LIKE YOUR HAIRCUT," Katherine said. "Shorter hair suits you."

"I thought it would be more age appropriate," Jessica said.

"Oh come on. Please don't tell me that was the main motivation for cutting your hair."

"Of course. Mid-forties means mid-length hair. Ask any woman in my family."

"If it's all the same to you, I'd rather not ask the women in your family anything at all—except you, of course."

They both chuckled.

"How are you feeling?" Katherine asked.

"Good," Jessica said. "Although there's something I've been meaning to ask you. Most likely something you're not too keen to talk about. But I can play the C-card, of course."

Katherine shook her head but had a grin on her face nonetheless. "You've played the C-card too often. It has lost its power."

"Damn." Jessica leaned back in her chair. "I thought I'd be able to use it for at least a year after my surgery."

"Maybe that works with other people, but not with me." Katherine put down her grapefruit mimosa. Jessica had invited her for brunch, although she wasn't partaking of the mimosas herself. Her doctor had advised her to not drink too much alcohol and, since her diagnosis, Jessica had drawn the line at daytime drinking. But it was good that Katherine already had two drinks down her. It would make her more amenable to the subject Jessica was eager to discuss.

Jessica looked her friend in the eye. There seemed to be no other way to ask this question, not for her. Eye contact was required. "What happened to Laurel?"

"Laurel?" Katherine said. "Why do you ask?"

Jessica rolled her eyes. "Why can't you simply answer a question with an actual reply instead of another question?"

"Come on, Jess. You know I can't give you any information about Laurel. We have a code of conduct."

"And is that code still valid once someone's no longer with the agency?"

Katherine sighed. "The truth is that I don't know what happened to Laurel after she quit. She's probably just living her life, like we all do, except she doesn't do certain things anymore." Katherine narrowed her eyes. "How do you know Laurel quit?"

"I, er, booked her for the other night. Someone else turned up."

Katherine's eyebrows shot up. "Are you serious?"

Jessica nodded slowly.

"God, Jess, I'm so sorry. That should never have happened."

"It worked out fine in the end."

"Did you make a complaint?"

"It's been dealt with."

Katherine tilted her head. "You're taking this surprisingly well."

"Believe me, I didn't at the time. But let's just say that the woman who turned up helped me change my mind over the course of the evening."

"Who was it?" Katherine asked.

"I'm not sure I'm allowed to say. Code of conduct and all that," Jessica said.

"The code doesn't apply to you," Katherine was quick to say.

"She called herself Liz. Probably not her real name. She didn't much look like a Liz."

Katherine nodded. "I know Liz."

"You do?" Jessica's heart skipped a beat.

"I like her. She's got a good sense of humor, which is a necessity in our line of work, although not everyone possesses the required amount. Liz does."

"Nothing happened," Jessica blurted out. "We just talked. Went for a walk."

Katherine looked at Jessica from under her lashes while she took another sip of her drink. "Would something have happened if Laurel had turned up?"

"Who's to say, really?" Jessica said wistfully. "I knew I wasn't ready but I wanted to force something. Now I'm not even sure I still want to use an escort agency to fulfill this need inside of me." She shook her head. "Sometimes I think having all this money has made me so fucked up in the head." Jessica was glad she could at least talk to Katherine about this. She wouldn't dream of broaching the subject with anyone else—not even someone as open-minded as Caitlin. It wasn't about the other person's open-mindedness anyway. It was about her own feelings of shame.

"Take it from someone who knows, Jess. For someone with too much money to know what to do with, you're a very decent person." Katherine grinned. "If you feel fucked up, it's because of the cancer. And the other stuff that happened before. The past few years have been rough on you."

"Is that an excuse to hire an escort, though?"

"You don't need an excuse. You don't need to justify yourself to *anyone*."

"Myself," Jessica said. "I had a lovely evening with Liz, but it was just that. An evening. God knows what she's doing with another woman right this moment. It's all so fake, yet it feels like all I'm capable of."

"It's not fake in the moment," Katherine said.

"I'm not sure I get what you're saying." Jessica looked at her friend. "You don't fake it with clients?"

"*You* are not faking it in the moment. What you feel is real. That's all that matters. That's why you asked Laurel to come over. Because, however briefly, you knew she could make you feel something real."

Jessica huffed out a breath. "I don't think so."

"Think about it for a day or two, then let me know if my words of wisdom still don't have a whiff of truth to them." Katherine found Jessica's gaze. "And don't forget, we have feelings too. We are humans just like you."

Jessica mixed Katherine another mimosa. Before she had cancer she wouldn't have dared to continue this line of questioning but since meeting Liz, her curiosity had been piqued. "Can I ask you something else?"

"You might as well. That's why you keep topping up my glass, isn't it? Although I would like to state for the record that it's no fun drinking alone. Won't you have a tiny glass with me? It's not going to kill you any faster, is it?"

Jessica burst out laughing. Comments like this were the very reason she and Katherine had become friends.

"Oh, all right." She quickly drank the contents of her water glass, poured a splash of champagne and a good glug of grapefruit juice into it, and held it up. "To tipsy Sunday brunches."

"And good friends." Katherine watched Jessica take a sip. "Now, shoot," she said. "What's the pressing matter on your mind?"

"Have you, um, ever developed feelings for a client?"

"I don't want to say you're easy to read, Jess, but I saw that one coming from a mile away." Katherine chuckled.

"How could you possibly have known what I was going to ask?"

"I see and hear so many things. A lot depends on me being able to read people. And you're my friend. I know you well." She drew her lips into a soft smile before speaking again. "And I couldn't help but notice the sparkle in your eyes when you spoke of Liz."

"What?" Jessica's cheeks flushed. "No, no, no. That's not why I'm asking." She drank from her mimosa. "And, once again, you're not answering the question."

"Okay, Little Miss Defensive... although I dare say the lady doth protest too much." She winked. "The answer to your question is no. This isn't *Pretty Woman*."

"Agreed. Not one Richard Gere in sight and thank goodness for that." Jessica fiddled with her hands. She regretted having asked the question—had she given away too much? To herself included?—yet she couldn't quite let it go. "You've never met anyone of who you thought that, under different circumstances you might hit it off with?"

"Ah, but that's the key right there. Circumstance is everything. I'm not saying emotions are that easily controlled all the time, or that it's the same for everyone, but I'm just not one to develop romantic feelings for someone who pays me money to sleep with them. There's a psychological line I can't cross, no matter how charming or nice or dazzling the client. It just doesn't happen. It's like, as a lesbian, you have to learn early on to not fall for the straight girls because you know there's just no way, and you know you'll only end up getting hurt."

"That didn't stop me from falling in love with many a straight girl in my time." Jessica scoffed.

"Yes well, hormones and puberty and such will do that to you. But now you know. You learned your lesson and you evolved. It's part of you."

"That just sounds a little too easy. Sometimes you simply can't help falling for a straight girl. If I had a penny for every adult lesbian hopelessly in love with a straight woman at this very moment, I'd be very rich indeed."

"You're rich already, Jess."

Jessica waved off Katherine's comment. "I don't agree with your analogy."

"It's a matter of give and take. Of giving the right signs. Or, if you're receiving signs that someone is developing a little crush, of not throwing oil onto the fire. And of being mature about these things."

"Let me ask you this then," Jessica said. "Have any of your clients had a noticeable crush on you?"

Katherine leaned back, taking her mimosa with her. After a while, she nodded. "It happens. It's a thin line when you spend time in bed with someone."

"How did you handle it?" Jessica's ears perked all the way up.

"Never by milking it, if that's what you're wondering." Katherine narrowed her eyes to slits.

"Who's defensive now?" Jessica asked.

"I'm just a bit baffled by your sudden curiosity about my job."

"I've always been this curious, Kat. I think before I was just too embarrassed to ask."

"But is it a coincidence that you want to know about it all

mere days after you met Liz?" Katherine quirked up her eyebrows.

"Yes and no." Jessica grinned at Katherine.

"Please elaborate."

"It had been months since I last saw Laurel. I had bloody surgery—I had a breast removed. My mind hasn't really been pondering the ins and outs of the escort service. Then meeting Liz, and having too much time on my hands, brought up a lot of questions. Does that explain it?"

"You could have had all those questions when you were a regular client of Laurel's. We were friends then. You could have asked me then."

"But that was before I knew I had cancer. Back then, I wasn't the type of person to ask questions like this."

"Ah, so if I understand correctly, your diagnosis, surgery, and convalescence have all worked together to ignite your curiosity about being a luxury escort. Are you considering a career switch, Jess?" Katherine had a smug smile on her face.

Jessica nearly spat out the sip of mimosa she just took. "Christ, imagine my father's reaction." She chuckled. "Or no, my stepmother's. Hers would be priceless. A drama for the ages. Woe her." She shook her head. "I'm just curious. That's it. And you *still* haven't answered my question."

"I'll answer more than your question." Katherine pushed a strand of hair behind her ear. "When I notice a client developing feelings for me, I wind down the relationship. That's the only correct way to deal with it. At least, that's the way *I* deal with it. I try not to embarrass them in the process and, if they're open to it, hook them up with someone else. It doesn't have to be a big drama." She leaned forward again, tapping her index finger onto the wooden table top. "Now as for the question you didn't ask—well, not in so many words, anyway." She tilted her head. "My conclusion is the following: I think you like Liz."

"Well, yes. I think I said as much." Jessica's hackles went all the way up.

"You sure did." Katherine extended her hand over the table and enveloped Jessica's in hers. "You're like an open book. I'm not saying this to goad you or embarrass you. I'm saying this as your friend. If this is how you feel after a few hours during which—your words—'nothing happened', I would advise you to not see Liz again. I can get you someone else. Someone more like Laurel."

"What?" Jessica shook her head. "No, Kat, you've got it all wrong. Those mimosas must have gone to your head." Jessica pushed a strand of hair behind her ear, but it was too short to remain there and sprang back immediately. Part of the reason why she'd had her hair cut shorter was because it no longer felt right to have long hair. When she went to the hospital to see her oncologist, the waiting room usually held a few people who had not been as fortunate to keep their hair during their treatment.

"I believe I can still hold my liquor." She drew her lips into a soft smile. "You're extra vulnerable right now. You crave someone's arms around you. It's a bitch what you've gone through—and you chose to do it alone, Jess. You didn't tell me you needed surgery. Your emotions were all over the place and you're only now coming back from that. I'm just trying to help. I don't want you to get hurt even more."

"The surgery was almost three months ago. I'm in a much better place right now."

"I can tell you're doing better physically. That's for sure." Katherine squeezed Jessica's hand. Jessica had to admit it felt good on hers. Just like feeling Liz's hand in hers had felt somehow right. "Often, when you feel better after an illness, the brain can trick you into feeling superhuman, like you're up for anything. But you need to give your emotions time to catch up. Falling in love with an escort isn't going to help that process."

Jessica drew her hand away. "For Christ's sake. I'm not falling in love with Liz. I've only met the woman once. All she turned out to be was a nice surprise." Jessica shook her head. "I know you mean well, but your powers of perception are not as finely attuned as you think they are."

Katherine held up her hands. "Fine. I'll drop it." She slanted herself away from Jessica. "Let's change the subject, shall we?"

"Let's." Jessica drank from her mimosa. She barely tasted the alcohol. It slid down so easily. She emptied her glass and poured herself another.

"Are you ready to go back to work?" Katherine asked.

"Oh yes. I'm so tired of doing nothing. That's what killed me after the agency went bankrupt as well. Waking up and having no idea what to do with my day."

"How's Caitlin?" A different kind of smile appeared on Katherine's face.

"She has been so kind to me. Truth be told, I hadn't expected it."

"Even after that disappearing act you pulled on her. Well, on both of us."

"Water under the bridge, Kat. You know why I did it. So does Caitlin. We've all moved on."

Katherine nodded. "When will you be ready to host another dinner party?" She quirked up one side of her mouth.

Jessica shook her head. "That ship has sailed. Caitlin and I are such good friends now."

"What does that say about our friendship then?" There was glee in Katherine's tone.

"It's different with you. Not every friendship is the same."

Katherine gave a brief chuckle then fell silent. "As soon

as you feel up to it, we should go to one of Jo's gigs. You haven't seen her live have you?"

"I've seen plenty of her live." Jessica couldn't help but smile.

"You know what I mean." Katherine smiled with her.

Jessica nodded. "I'll let you know."

Chapter Six

"MORTON'S FINE," Caitlin said. "Very unintrusive." She was referring to the person currently replacing Jessica at ANBC while she was on sick leave.

"You mean he doesn't nag you about getting certain people on your show?" When Jessica had just started her job at the network and had become Caitlin's boss, she had pushed relentlessly for Caitlin to interview reality TV star Kathy Kramer. The show had been a disaster. Jessica had learned her lesson and had since refrained from suggesting guests.

"There's that." Caitlin beamed a wide smile at her. "How are you feeling?" She sipped from her coffee. They were sitting at a table by the window in the Pink Bean.

"Fine." One of the oddest experiences of falling ill was not being able to resort to that standard reply whenever someone asked how she was doing. It was a word so ingrained in everyday life, it was hard to deviate from, even when she was feeling at her worst.

"Really?" Caitlin insisted. "You know you can talk to me."

"Do I not look fine to you?" Jessica painted on a fake, wide grin.

"You do. You look remarkable for someone on sick leave."

"That's why I'm going back to work next week. I've missed bugging you."

"Oh, and how we've missed you." Caitlin put her cup down.

"It does feel a bit strange, though," Jessica said. "It doesn't feel like the same person going back. Honestly, I got lucky. Yes, I had surgery, but it wasn't even that invasive—"

Caitlin held up her hand. "Let me stop you right there." She leaned over the table. "You keep doing this, Jess. You keep claiming you got lucky and that it could have been much worse. But you had a breast removed. You had cancer. That's not what's generally considered 'being lucky.'"

"Not everyone gets to survive," Jessica said.

"That's true, but that doesn't mean you're not allowed to feel shaken up by this whole thing."

"I feel plenty shaken up." Jessica took a deep breath. "I'm just over having to talk about it all the time." She ran a finger over the handle of her coffee cup. "Yet I'm constantly reminded of it. Not only when I can't face myself in the mirror, but just in everyday life. For example, when I think about going back to work. I think in terms of pre- and post-cancer now. I'm not really sure who I am post-cancer, while I knew very well who I was before."

"Let me tell you how your co-workers saw you before cancer," Caitlin said, keeping her voice low.

"No need. They saw me as the big boss's daughter. A bit of a tough bitch who was out to prove she was more than a daddy's girl who took one of the top jobs. Not on merit, but because of nepotism."

"Wow," Caitlin said on a sigh. "Seems to me you've

become even harder on yourself." She shook her head. "That's not what I was going to say at all."

Jessica let her shoulders slump. She inhaled deeply to regroup. "It's like there's this dark cloud following me around. It doesn't always hang over my head, but it moves in and out. When it does move in, things always look so bleak."

"Do you think coming back to work will help?" Caitlin asked.

Jessica nodded vigorously. "God, yes. I need some purpose."

"You won't be working full-time from the get-go, will you?" Caitlin pinned her gaze on Jessica.

"No, but not because I don't want to. They won't let me. My father must have gotten to the HR department. It's very unlike him to meddle with things like that."

"Maybe he realized he could have lost you."

Jessica scoffed. "Edward Porter doesn't let his mind become occupied with futilities like that."

"You'd be surprised," Caitlin said.

"And you're the expert on parents now, are you?" Jessica was well aware of how acerbic she sounded.

"Christ, Jess," Caitlin said. "You have a wall of sarcasm of about this thick around you." Caitlin held her hands ten inches apart. "I know why, so I forgive you, but when you go back to work, not everyone will be as understanding as I am." Caitlin looked at the door and her face lit up.

Jessica followed her gaze. Jo had just walked in. Jessica hadn't seen her often since the night they'd spent together, but every time she did a shiver ran up her spine.

She had orchestrated that night when she, Caitlin, Jo and Katherine had landed in bed together for a reason. It was meant to be a farewell to the Jessica with two naturally-grown breasts. Seeing Jo reminded her very specifically of that, because that night Jo had definitely been the most taken with her breasts. What would she think if she saw them now?

"I'm sorry," Jessica quickly mumbled. Caitlin had sat by her bedside when Jessica hadn't been able to do much and had confided in her about her own sour relationship with her parents.

Caitlin waved her off. "You're forgiven." She pulled up a chair for Jo.

"Hey, Jess," Jo said, and leaned down to kiss Jessica on the cheek. "You're looking well."

"Coffee with Caitlin James will do that to you," Jessica replied. She shot Jo a quick wink, then scanned Caitlin's face to make sure she had definitely been forgiven for her earlier remark.

Jo put an arm around Caitlin's shoulders. "Refills?" Jo glanced around the Pink Bean. "I haven't worked here in months yet it still feels strange to just walk in here," she said.

"Decaf for me, please," Jessica said. "I think this is around the time Amber comes in and I don't want another lecture on the negative effects of caffeine on my body's healing process."

"Even Amber can't tell the difference between regular coffee and decaf by sight alone," Jo said.

Jessica shrugged. "Then I guess her speech worked on me, because I'll have decaf regardless."

"If you really wanted to impress her, you'd have a green tea," Caitlin chimed in.

"And go vegan," Jo added. She glanced at Caitlin. "Another long black for you, babe, so you'll be nicely jacked up for the rest of the day?"

Caitlin patted Jo on the back. "You got it."

Jo headed to the counter and Jessica took the opportunity to lean over the table and say, "Katherine asked about you the other day."

Caitlin pursed her lips together and nodded. "How is she?"

"She wanted to know when I would be throwing another dinner party *like that.*" Jessica couldn't help but grin.

Caitlin chuckled. "What did you say?"

"That you and I are friends of a different nature now."

Caitlin nodded. "I'm glad we agree."

They sat in silence for a few moments.

"That doesn't mean we can't have a meal together, of course," Caitlin said after a while. "Do you want to come to ours some time? Bring Katherine?"

"That would be lovely." Jessica couldn't help but think about someone else she would like to bring. After her conversation with Katherine, Jessica had tried not to think about Liz, but trying not to think about someone usually had the opposite result. Jessica's brain was subject to the same laws of psychology. She thought about her evening with Liz often. She tried berating herself by replaying Katherine's words in her head, but she always ended up rebuffing them. What Katherine had claimed was simply too ludicrous.

Jo returned with their cups of coffee.

"Tell us when you're free, darling," Caitlin said, "Jess and Katherine are coming to dinner."

Jo quirked up her eyebrows but didn't say anything.

"Not like that," Caitlin said. "Just dinner."

Jo chuckled. "Of course. What else could we possibly do but eat, drink, and be merry?"

Chapter Seven

JESSICA'S first day back at work wasn't going so well. She felt almost as out of place as she had on the day her own company had gone bust and she hadn't told any of her employees yet. Today, she felt like someone placed by her father to oversee the Programming Department, like a mere puppet drilled to report on any unusual goings-on, not someone capable of actually running the department. Caitlin had been right, Morton had done a good job of replacing her. Apart from going through a mailbox with too many emails in it to ever read, Jessica didn't quite know what to do with herself.

Instead of addressing her inbox and getting back into the swing of things, she picked up her phone and scrolled through the apps. Her finger eventually landed on the web browser in which she opened a private window. She logged on to the escort agency's website and let her finger hover over the contact button. Her pulse picked up speed. Katherine had been right about one thing. The entire process at least made Jessica feel very much alive—made her feel something real.

The required action was simple. All she had to do was send a message and request Liz. It could be as brief as 'Liz - this afternoon - my known address'.

But Jessica closed the browser window and threw her phone onto her desk. She had work to do. She shot out of her chair and walked to the window. From her office she could see Darling Harbour. Dozens of tiny people were milling about below, going about their day. They walked as though filled to the brim with a sense of purpose. Something Jessica couldn't possibly fathom.

But what had she expected? That she could just step into her office and, as though she had walked through a magic door, she would feel that drive again?

She didn't feel any purpose, nor magic. It was like she had lost all the drive she had started this new job with not even a year ago. The truth was that while she was on sick leave, Jessica had barely watched ANBC, or any other network TV. The only exception was *The Caitlin James Show*.

She had blamed it on her illness, on not having much appetite for anything. Watching TV had been very low on her list of needs to fulfill, even if it was the only thing to keep her company, especially during the long hours before and after midnight. She had believed this was because TV just reminded her of work, and work reminded her of her advertising agency that she had led into bankruptcy, and the fallout of all of that.

But now that she was back at work, she didn't feel that spark she used to feel anymore. She didn't know if it was because some of her views on life had changed since her diagnosis, or simply because she was, as her father would most likely call it, capricious.

"You're in your forties, yet you behave like one of those entitled millennials," he'd said after he had paid off her employees—his money in return for their silence.

Jessica shook off that thought and tried to empty her mind the way Amber had taught her. Caitlin had brought her on a few visits while she was convalescing, even though they hardly knew each other. Caitlin had barely been able to stop Amber from going through Jessica's kitchen cabinets searching for foods that should be in no cancer survivor's pantry.

Jessica closed off her right nostril with her thumb, breathed in deeply through the other, then pushed her index finger against her left nostril and exhaled through the right one. This was supposed to calm her down. The problem was that Jessica wasn't feeling agitated. It was more a sense of total deflation that absorbed her.

She'd been scared of coming back to work, but also excited. Now that she was here however, the same numbness that had lain over her like a blanket since her surgery had returned—a blanket that she couldn't throw off, no matter how hard she tried.

The only time she'd felt it lift, was on that walk with Liz. And when Liz had pushed her thumbs into the hard knots underneath Jessica's shoulder blades.

Jessica checked her watch. It was almost eleven. She was only supposed to be in half a day. She'd had a big breakfast meeting with the key people in her department earlier that morning. She'd been briefed but, she got the impression, not too much. Even the people she worked with felt like she wasn't fully back yet. She could leave work right now and no one would care. A few people would notice, but they would shrug it off all too easily.

The fact of the matter was that Jessica didn't want to be there. She wanted to walk around the city, preferably with Liz on her arm. Was that really such a bad thing to want? Perhaps it was exactly what she needed. Some time with Liz to recharge and start fresh at work tomorrow. Yes, that was it.

She could come in the next day feeling more alive, ready and able.

She walked to her desk, picked up her phone, and opened the private browser window again. She sent the message.

She paced through her office waiting for a response after the immediate automated one. Was someone calling Liz now to check her availability—and her willingness to see Jessica again? Jessica had been glad for the opportunity to quiz Katherine, but she still had so many questions left. Maybe she could ask Liz. She just wanted to go for a walk, maybe get another one of those shoulder massages, and have a chat.

And feel the warmth of Liz's smile.

She glared at her phone every few seconds, but refused to let herself pick it up until ten minutes had passed. What if Liz didn't want to see her anymore? Or if Katherine had told her about their conversation. Was that even possible? Wouldn't that break the agency's code of conduct?

She picked up her phone and checked her messages on the website. A new one had come in.

Liz will be at your known address at 3:00 p.m.

Jessica balled her fist in a gesture of victory. Instantly, the apathy she had been drenched in all morning fell away. She had four hours to get ready for Liz.

Chapter Eight

JESSICA WAS ready long before Liz rang the doorbell. A little before three, she heard a car pull up in her quiet street. A door opened and closed, then the car drove off. She wondered if the agency had their own car service or if they just used taxis and Ubers.

She opened the door before Liz had a chance to ring the bell. Jessica scanned the street, but her gaze was instantly drawn to Liz.

"Hey." Liz stood there grinning, as though it had always been a foregone conclusion that Jessica would request her services again.

"Hi, please come in." Jessica gave Liz a once-over. She was slightly taken aback by her outfit. Laurel would never have shown up in jeans—no matter how well-fitted—and a plaid shirt. Jessica could distinguish fine clothing from cheap garments made in Asian factories, and the shirt Liz was wearing, unbuttoned over a white, very tight top, didn't look cheap at all, yet the way she wore it made her look so casual. Too casual for the job she was here to do.

Liz slipped inside and as she walked past, Jessica could

smell her perfume. It was fruity and light with a hint of nut. Liz halted in the hallway and put a hand on Jessica's shoulder. "Good to see you again," she said.

"You too." Jessica let her gaze linger on Liz's jeans for an instant and slanted her head.

Liz looked Jessica in the eye. "This is how I dress on a Monday. I took a gamble and thought you'd be okay with that."

Jessica arched up her eyebrows. "It's fine, of course." She tried very hard to not look for any deeper meaning behind Liz's choice of clothing even though it didn't align with her idea of how an escort was supposed to dress.

"How are you?" Liz asked and squeezed Jessica's shoulder again.

"Well." She led them into the living room. "I was hoping we could go for a walk again. The weather's lovely."

Liz stuck out a foot. "Sensible shoes." They were brown leather boots. The color matched Liz's belt. She wore a leather jacket in a slightly darker shade of brown. If Jessica had crossed her in the street looking like this, she wouldn't have only turned around because Liz was a beautiful woman, but because her gaydar would be seriously pinging.

She couldn't wait to walk through the streets of Pott's Point with this woman on her arm.

"Didn't you say you were starting work again this week?" Liz asked.

They had walked to the end of Jessica's street in silence. Jessica wondered if Liz needed some time to read her mood before she initiated conversation. Or perhaps she didn't really know what to say. Conversation skills were surely something she needed in her line of work, but,

Jessica figured, it was hardly her main job. Or maybe it was.

Too many questions were buzzing around in her head again, so she was glad Liz broke the silence, even if it meant she had to talk about work.

"I did, I started today. Only part-time for the first few weeks though. We'll see how it goes."

"How did it go this morning?" Liz was the one to steer them to the right at the end of the street. It didn't matter which direction they walked in. Jessica just wanted to be outside of her house, breathe in some fresh air, and not feel alone while doing so.

Jessica shook her head. "Not an unequivocal success." Her shoulders slumped at the mere memory of how deflated she had felt.

"Isn't that to be expected after a long absence?" Liz asked.

"No, I was expecting the opposite." Jessica glanced at Liz from the corner of her eye.

"Maybe you went back too soon."

"Maybe," Jessica mumbled, but her mind had been put on a different track already. "Have you ever had a corporate job?" she asked.

Liz remained silent for a beat. "I have." Silence again. Jessica didn't say anything, hoping Liz would continue of her own accord. "It was an office job. I would hardly call it corporate. Admin mostly. It didn't suit me very much." She turned to Jessica and smiled. "Come to think of it, it was kind of soul-sucking. And the money wasn't all that good either."

"Soul-sucking?" Jessica repeated.

"It was just dreary, unchallenging, repetitive office work. Some people can thrive in that sort of environment, but I can't."

"Soul-sucking is not a word you would use to describe your current job?" Jessica asked.

"No way." Liz vehemently shook her head. "Quite the opposite I would say."

"Really?"

Liz stopped in her tracks. "It's kind of a strange question."

It was physically impossible for Jessica not to look up to Liz as they stood facing each other.

"Does any of this feel soul-sucking to you?" Liz asked.

"Well, no, but I—"

"You're the client." Liz grinned. "And there's a distinct difference between us in this relationship." She crossed her arms in front of her chest. "That's absolutely true, but I never do a job I don't want to do."

Her words reminded Jessica that, in the end, that was all she was and ever could be to Liz: a job.

Liz uncrossed her arms and touched a finger to Jessica's chin. "I'm out and about on a beautiful spring day with a gorgeous, sophisticated woman. Tell me where the bad deal in that is for me?" She tilted up Jessica's chin.

Jessica averted her eyes. A hot flush crept up her cheeks. Gorgeous? Sophisticated? Technically, Liz was paid to say these things to her, but that didn't mean she had to.

"Shall we continue our walk?" Jessica said.

"Let's go." Liz offered Jessica her arm again, and Jessica gladly hooked hers through.

They walked in silence for a while and Jessica managed to quieten the voice in her head and just enjoy the simple sensation of, as Liz had called it, being out and about. She reveled in the sound of Liz's footsteps next to her, totally in step with her own. In the looks that Liz drew from passersby because of her height and her stunning face.

Jessica let Liz guide the way. Since this was her neighborhood, her walks always took her in the same direction as a force of habit. Liz's meanderings had brought them to the edge of Darlinghurst. Jessica could see the top of Caitlin's building from where she stood.

"Would you like a cup of coffee?" she asked.

"I would love one."

"I know just the place," Jessica said.

———

"I'll get the coffees," Liz said after they had walked into the Pink Bean. "You sit down."

"Are you sure?" Again, Jessica was flummoxed by Liz's behavior. Wasn't the client supposed to provide all beverages?

"Of course." Liz shot Jessica a wide grin.

"Okay." Jessica found a table by the window. She looked around, but didn't see anyone familiar. It was the middle of the afternoon.

Jessica's gaze was drawn to Liz's backside as she stood at the counter. She filled out those jeans in the most exquisite way. Jessica couldn't even picture Liz in a dress. She couldn't be totally sure, of course, but she believed Liz wasn't only gay for pay. There was too distinct a feeling she couldn't shake off.

If only she could have ten minutes of unlimited question time. But inside information was much harder to come by than other things when dealing with women like Liz and Katherine. At least that was how they made it look.

"A double espresso for you." Liz arrived at the table. "Planning to stay up late, are you?" She winked at Jessica then sat down opposite and held up her cup. "I'm more a soft-core latte girl myself."

They sipped from their beverages. As Jessica put her cup down, she asked, "How many hours did you exercise today?"

"A grand total of zero," Liz said. "I got an unexpected call."

"Oh yes." Jessica nodded. "A demanding customer."

"Not in the least." Liz smiled softly.

"So…" Jessica was already mentally preparing for a rebuff, but she wanted to ask the question nonetheless. "How does it work when I send a message on the agency's website?"

Liz narrowed her eyes. "Up until now you've been someone who wants to know everything about what I do rather than enjoy my services."

"Right now, that is a very accurate impression of me."

"Okay." Liz nodded. "I'll answer your questions, but I would like to ask you for something in return."

"Sure." Something inside Jessica lit up.

"Two things, actually, because I'm going to need your discretion as well."

"That goes without saying."

Liz gave a curt nod. "You won't let me leave without having given you a shoulder massage again." She plastered a wide smile on her lips.

"How can I say no to a smile like that?" Maybe this was what Jessica had missed most of all. Flirting. Innuendo. The deliciously promising back and forth between her and another woman.

Liz bit her lip. She excelled at the game of seduction whereas Jessica was feeling a little rusty.

"To answer your question, when someone sends a message requesting me and the requested time slot is free in the calendar I share with the agency, I get a call."

"So there's always someone monitoring the messages coming in?"

"Of course. We provide a non-stop service."

"On very short notice as well, it would appear."

"Only the best for our clients. We're as high-end and niche as you can get."

"What does that really mean?" Now this was interesting, unlike the latest ratings analysis of a TV show Jessica didn't much care about.

"It means that there aren't that many women who have the means to pay the prices we charge for 'The Lesbian Experience'."

Jessica rolled her eyes. "That name almost put me off. Who the hell came up with that?"

"Not a lesbian." Liz's cheeks dimpled as she burst into a chuckle. "So despite being put off by our name, what pulled you over the edge?" Liz rested her chin on an upturned palm and regarded Jessica intently.

"A friend of mine who works for The Lesbian Experience."

"Really?"

Jessica nodded.

"You're not going to tell me who?" Liz asked.

"I don't know. I don't want to break any protocol."

"You won't be breaking anything if you say who it is, I assure you."

"To me, she's Katherine. I believe she goes by Lucy at the agency." Jessica felt like she was doing something illicit by mentioning Katherine's real name.

"That just goes to show," Liz said. "We have friends too." She shot Jessica one of her irresistible smiles again.

"Katherine's one of the only friends who has stood by me through all the shit that has happened the past few years. The cancer. My company going bust. The woman I loved leaving me at the worst time. She's one in a million."

"So you didn't meet her through the agency?"

"No. I met her at one of my father's charity balls. She was the plus one of a guest. Turned quite a few heads, as you can imagine. She mainly made my gaydar ping. We got talking and hit it off."

"Interesting." Liz pouted her lips.

"Why are you looking at me like that?" Jessica asked.

"No reason. I'm just trying to picture the scene." She grinned briefly. "That's something I like to do when someone tells me a story."

"When she told me what she did for a living, my interest was… rather piqued," Jessica said. She had never told this to anyone, not even Caitlin. "Do you tell your friends what you do for a living?"

"Not everyone." Liz sat up a little straighter. "I'd like to be all if-they-can't-accept-what-I-do-we're-not-really-friends about it, but that's not how it works. It's not as black and white. Some people just can't deal with what I do. I accept that. I have no choice. But most of my friends know. The closest ones at least. But I never give them any details about my day, of course."

"I hope not."

"We sign very strict non-disclosure agreements. My discretion is literally worth hundreds of thousands of dollars."

"How about your parents?" Jessica asked.

Liz didn't immediately reply. She looked through the window for a brief moment, then back at Jessica. "My mother died nine years ago. She never knew. My father is… Well, he doesn't have a problem with it. He doesn't have a problem with much of anything. He's the very definition of laid back."

"I'm sorry to hear about your mother." Jessica sipped from her cup but her coffee had gone cold.

Liz nodded slowly. She opened her mouth to speak, but then closed it again. She looked away again and only glanced at Jessica after several moments had passed. "I always think I can't say this to other cancer patients, which is bullshit, in the end." She held Jessica's gaze. "My mother died of ovarian cancer."

An ice-cold arrow shot up Jessica's spine. "I'm so sorry," she managed to say.

"Thankfully, I'm not here to talk about my mother." The smile Liz drew her lips into wasn't very convincing.

"You can if you want to. I mean, you don't have to refrain from saying anything because I have—*had* cancer." Jessica stared at the remaining coffee in her cup. "I can handle it, if that's what you're worried about."

"I know you can." Liz startled her by finding Jessica's hand on the table and covering it with hers.

Jessica's gut reaction was to look around and check again whether anyone she knew was at the Pink Bean. Liz might not be dressed the part, but her actions could give certain things away that Jessica would prefer to keep hidden. Then again, that hand felt good on hers, warm and comforting, and she was the one who had wanted to take Liz out.

"Can I speak frankly?" Liz asked, giving Jessica's hand another squeeze.

Jessica nodded slowly. "I guess."

"Yes or no." Liz's smile had become genuine again.

"Yes." The strong tone with which Liz asked the question sent a frisson of excitement through Jessica.

"I think you can handle a hell of a lot more than you think you can at this moment."

Jessica scanned Liz's face. She lost her focus on what Liz had just said for a split second, simply because her features were too mesmerizing. "Maybe," was all Jessica said. "I just don't feel like doing a whole lot."

"I get that, but…" Liz fell silent.

"But what?" Jessica leaned onto the table.

"Look, you don't know me and you don't have any

reason to trust me, but I'd like to take you home and show you what you're capable of."

Jessica's cheeks broke into an instant flush. What was Liz insinuating? "Wh-what do you mean?"

"You'll see when we get there," Liz said and waggled her eyebrows.

Chapter Nine

WHEN THEY ARRIVED at Jessica's house, Liz halted in the hallway and gazed at a painting hanging on the wall. "I probably don't have to tell you," she said, "but this is worth a small fortune."

Jessica stood next to her and looked at the painting with her. "You know more than I do."

Liz looked at her, her brows knitted together. "This is a Robert Barrow. They go for at least a million at auction."

"I hadn't pegged you for an art buff."

"Art historian, actually," Liz said. "The most useless degree you can get at university, but I do recognize a Barrow when I see one."

"You studied Art History?" Jessica took a step back and regarded Liz the way they'd just been studying the painting.

"Is that so surprising?" Liz's smile turned into a lopsided grin.

"I don't know. It surprised *me*." Jessica huffed out an awkward giggle.

Liz leaned against the hallway cabinet, seemingly no longer interested in the painting. "What I'm wondering is, if you have all this money hanging on your walls, why did your company go bust? Why didn't you just pay off the debts and move on?"

Instinctively, Jessica took a step back. "That's a very direct question."

"Is it?" Liz jutted out her bottom lip. "I didn't think it was."

"I'd rather not talk about that if it's all the same to you."

Liz took a step closer. "Your wish is my command."

This made Jessica chuckle. "What did you want to show me?"

"I'd like *you* to start by showing me your bedroom." Liz squared her impressive shoulders.

"I—I'm not sure I want to—"

"Just show me. That's all I ask. I'd like to give you a proper back massage. Nothing more."

Jessica considered this for a moment. She did want to feel Liz's hands on her skin again. She was just worried about what she meant by a *proper* massage. Jessica could hazard a guess, of course.

"Okay," Jessica said and headed up the stairs. Liz followed on her heels.

"Welcome to my boudoir." Jessica opened the bedroom door.

"This should work." Liz scanned the room, then looked at Jessica. "Can you lie on your belly comfortably, or would you prefer a pillow underneath you?"

"I'm fine." It had taken a while, but she could finally sleep on her belly again.

"Do you mind taking off your blouse and lying face down for me? I'll be getting ready in the bathroom while you do so. I won't see anything you don't want me to see. Only your back. Leave your bra on if it makes you feel more secure."

"You don't mess about, do you?" Jessica said.

"Sometimes that's what it takes." Liz flashed her a smile, then pointed at the door next to the bed. "Is that a bathroom?"

Jessica nodded.

"I'll be in there. Just give me a shout when you're ready."

Before she went into the bathroom, Liz stepped closer and cupped Jessica's jaw in her hand. "It's going to be all right, Jess." She said it as though no truer words had ever been spoken. Only Jessica's friends abbreviated her name and it made her feel, for a split second, as though she was in the company of a friend.

Liz dropped her hand and strutted into the bathroom. Jessica stared at the closed door for a few seconds. She took a deep breath. Taking off her blouse was not a problem for her when she was alone and there was no mirror around. She unbuttoned it and hung it over a chair. She debated whether to take off her bra, but that debate quickly fizzled out when she thought of the glimpses she had caught of herself in the mirror, and all the times she had turned away from her mirror image.

She drew the line at her bra. She kept it on and lay on the bed. She let herself sink into the mattress and allowed herself the moment of delightful anticipation. There was nothing to be afraid of. And there was a gorgeous woman getting ready—whatever that entailed—in her bathroom to give her a back massage.

"I'm ready," Jessica said. She didn't know if it was loud enough for Liz to hear, but sure enough, a few moments later, Liz exited the bathroom. She carried a small bottle of oil and a towel and she was no longer wearing the shirt over her top, revealing toned arms. And a smile so disarming, Jessica was sorry she was lying on her belly because it would be taken from her view any moment now.

Liz didn't comment on Jessica still wearing her bra. She proceeded in silence. She covered everything below the fastening of Jessica's bra with the towel, then, gently, Jessica felt Liz straddle her. She didn't rest any of her weight on Jessica but Jessica felt her jeans-clad knees against her sides where the towel didn't cover her completely.

"Actually," Liz said, and pushed herself up carefully. "I'm going to take these off."

Jessica watched Liz slip out of her jeans. The skin she bared looked so smooth, Jessica had to resist the urge to reach out and run a finger over Liz's thigh. But before she knew it, Liz was straddling her again, this time with her bare knees touching the naked skin of Jessica's. Jessica didn't protest or draw Liz's attention to the towel in disarray.

She heard the same squirting sound she'd heard the first evening with Liz, then the rubbing of oily palms together. Next, a pair of warm hands landed on her shoulders. Liz caressed her only lightly, spreading the oil.

"Can I move these out of the way?" she whispered as she hooked a finger underneath Jessica's bra strap.

"Okay." Jessica was hardly going to resist now. And why did her voice sound so hoarse?

Liz lowered her bra straps. Jessica maneuvered her arms out of them one at a time, making sure the cups of her bra remained in place.

Liz gently tucked the straps under the top of the towel. She spread some oil on Jessica's neck and Jessica felt all the tiny hairs on her body stand up. She already had to catch her breath and the massage hadn't even started yet.

As she moved her hand about Jessica's neck and shoulders, Liz's behind sometimes touched down lightly on Jessica's.

Jessica wished she could see Liz's biceps flex as she

worked on her body. If only she could turn around, but that was still out of the question.

"Aah," Jessica moaned when Liz pushed her thumbs into the sensitive spots on her shoulders. Then she simply gave in to the myriad of sensations engulfing her. Relaxation was one of them, but there were many others. She was much more aware of Liz's touch on her skin this time around. Liz's hands moved around much more freely and, Jessica believed, with much more abandon.

Liz's breath sounded steady and controlled. The pressure of her kneading motions gradually increased until Jessica believed she didn't have a single ounce of tension left in her shoulder muscles.

Liz's hands stopped moving and Jessica felt her breath pass along her ear.

"I'm going to move the towel down a little," she said.

She didn't ask. She just told Jessica what she was going to do. Maybe she sensed Jessica would say yes—she'd agree to just about anything at this point.

Soon after, the towel slid down Jessica's back. Liz ran a finger down her spine and the sensation coaxed another moan, albeit of a slightly different nature, from Jessica's throat.

Again, without asking, Liz unfastened her bra. She did it slowly, gently sliding the sides onto the bed. Jessica stiffened a bit in response, but she told herself to take a deep breath. That particular piece of fabric hadn't been hiding anything vital—it just stood in the way of more pleasure.

Liz spread more oil onto Jessica's back and repeated the same process as before. She started by simply caressing Jessica's skin, incrementally upping the pressure, until her fingertips drained Jessica's body of all the tension she'd been keeping inside.

Jessica was so relaxed, she allowed her mind to drift to

where she had fiercely forbidden it to go before. What if Liz had been Laurel? Would more have happened? Would she have shown herself already? And what would it be like to be touched like that by Liz? What was Liz's real name? There were so many boundaries she wanted to cross, but she wouldn't get anywhere if she failed to take on the first hurdle.

When the back massage was finished, Liz leaned over her and pushed Jessica's hair away from her ear. "Any other spots you would like me to get my hands on?" Her voice was sultry and deep.

Jessica took a moment to consider her reply. She had sort of expected the question. She twisted her neck as far as it would go in her current position. "Yes," she said.

Liz nodded and slowly moved off her, as though not to disturb the delicate balance in the atmosphere between them. She lay down on her side, looking at Jessica's face.

"Take all the time you need," she whispered.

Chapter Ten

JESSICA GLANCED into Liz's eyes, as though all the strength she needed for what she was about to do could be found in the depths of them.

She started by pushing herself up with one arm. Her left side—the intact one—would become visible first. She moved her bra from underneath her and tossed it to the side. Ever so slowly, Jessica started to turn on her side to face Liz, covering her chest as best she could with her arm, still limp from the massage. She stopped when she came eye to eye with Liz, who kept her gaze firmly on Jessica's face.

Her right side was covered by the arm she held in front of it.

Liz raised her hand and with the lightest touch imaginable, stroked Jessica's left arm. "You're so brave," she said.

It was all Jessica needed to reach the next level of courage. Those words from Liz.

As she turned onto her back, Liz's hand slipped onto Jessica's belly, and stayed there. The physical connection between them strengthened Jessica's resolve. She was doing this. There was no mirror anywhere near her. She wouldn't even have to see it herself.

Jessica lay on her back, her arms crossed over her chest.

Liz's hand was warm and comforting on her belly. She'd pushed herself onto an elbow and wore a gentle smile on her lips. She looked deep into Jessica's eyes. She started moving her hand. Just her fingers really, wiggling them about a bit. One started tracing a circle around her belly button. Jessica's remaining nipple reacted instantly. It pressed against the flesh of the arm covering her breast.

Then, out of nowhere, or so it seemed to her, she said, "Kiss me, please."

Liz's eyes narrowed, then closed, as she brought her face forward and gently placed her lips on Jessica's. Jessica's body responded by relaxing into the mattress. Another woman's lips on hers. It had been too long. She had pushed too many people away. She'd become afraid of everything, of the smallest, most ridiculous things, as well as the delicious plea- sure of kissing another person.

Liz removed her hand from Jessica's belly and brought it to Jessica's neck, her fingers caressing her jaw. Their tongues slipped into each other's mouths and, as they did, Jessica lowered her arms. She freed her chest from the cage she had kept it in. Her nipple stiffened more in response.

She threw an arm around Liz's waist. No matter how good that top looked on her, she wanted to yank it off her. Her other hand she used to draw Liz's face closer toward hers, to drink more of her in. She tasted so good. She smelled divine. Her flesh felt hard and toned underneath Jessica's touch. Jessica was getting so carried away, she nearly forgot about how she got here in the first place. Until they broke from their kiss.

She smiled up at Liz and kept her arms where they were, away from her chest.

Liz caressed her cheek. "You set the pace."

"Seems to me you're rather good at that, actually," Jessica replied.

"In that case, I most certainly wouldn't mind you asking me to kiss you again," Liz said, her voice low and sexy.

Jessica glanced at Liz's shoulder line and the strong arms coming out of the sleeves of her T-shirt. She never wanted Liz to wear anything else again. Then she shut down that line of thought because it reminded her too much of how Liz had come to lie next to her in bed, about to kiss her again.

"Kiss me," Jessica said.

Liz leaned in again and pressed Jessica into the pillow a bit deeper this time. Her body didn't push all the way down onto Jessica's, but it was mere millimeters away. The kiss was less exploratory, more brazen. Liz's fingers cupped Jessica's jaw with a bit more vigor. This woman wasn't about to treat her like a delicate doll—the way Jessica had been treating herself.

Jessica brought her hand underneath Liz's top and reveled in the smooth touch of her skin, before giving in to the urge to take that T-shirt off her. She pushed it upward to make her wishes known. Liz withdrew from the kiss and grinned at her.

"I like the pace you're setting, Jess," she said, found some balance, and proceeded to hoist the T-shirt over her head.

Jessica swallowed hard as she came face to face with Liz's near-naked torso. Bloody hell. What was it she said she did? *T-Rex?* Jessica wondered if she could sign up to watch from the sidelines while Liz worked on her muscles. Whatever it was she was doing, it was working a charm.

Jessica let her finger drift over Liz's skin. She explored slowly, letting the sensations wash over her. It was only after a few minutes of doing so, that she realized she had left her right side totally exposed.

But Jessica didn't stop exploring Liz's skin with her fingers to cover herself up. Feeling Liz's soft flesh against hers was so much more powerful than the fear that kept her from showing herself.

Her hand reached Liz's breast and when she stroked her nipple through the fabric of Liz's bra, it rose to meet her touch.

"This is going to have to come off, I think," she said.

"Why don't you help me with that?" Liz shot her a grin, then maneuvered over Jessica to give her easy access to the clasp of her bra. Jessica unfastened it and guided the bra off Liz's body.

"There we are," she said, her gaze drawn to Liz's breasts. Just like Liz, to Jessica, they looked perfect. Unblemished. Small, tight nipples. A creamy roundness to them she wanted to discover more of. Jessica couldn't bring herself to touch them. While Liz's bra had still covered her breasts, it hadn't been a problem, but now she suddenly felt incapable of bringing her hands to them.

"I used to have beautiful breasts," Jessica said, without the slightest touch of self-pity in her voice. "I was never one of those women who grew up hating my body."

"Do you hate your body now?" Liz asked. She shuffled a little closer and lay down on her side, facing Jessica.

"Hate is a strong word." Jessica sought Liz's hand and intertwined her fingers with hers. "It just feels so out of balance, which makes it feel not right. Makes *me* feel not right."

"You're still a gorgeous woman," Liz said. "Take it from me."

Jessica scoffed.

"You *are*." Liz brought her face closer and kissed Jessica

on the nose. She planted another soft kiss on her cheek, then found her lips. When they broke from the brief kiss, Liz drew a path along Jessica's neck, to her ear. "You're so hot. You turn me on," she whispered. She kissed Jessica's neck again. She planted light kisses along the length of it while her words buzzed around Jessica's head.

You turn me on.

Was it a trick of the trade?

What else could it possibly be?

Liz's kisses trailed down. She kissed the swell of Jessica's left breast, then looked at her. "Is this okay?" she asked.

Jessica hesitated. "Give me a second."

"Of course." Liz let herself fall onto the bed next to Jessica.

"No, stay where you are. Please. Tell me what you see."

Liz quirked up her eyebrows, but then followed Jessica's instructions. She lowered her gaze and looked at Jessica's chest.

"Tell me," Jessica whispered.

Liz cleared her throat. "I see a beautiful breast with a terribly erect nipple." She briefly looked up and smiled at Jessica. "And I see a scar. Like this." With her finger she drew a half-moon in the air. "Like a smile, actually."

"How off-putting is it?" Jessica asked. Her arousal levels had dropped and had been replaced by renewed anxiety.

"It's not off-putting at all, Jess."

"It's hardly a turn on, though."

"It's who you are now. It's a testament to what you've gone through. Of your survival. It's powerful that way." Liz looked at her and cocked her head. "Do you want to see?" She threw in a smile. "Maybe because you've been so afraid to look, you've blown it out of proportion in your head. I'm telling you, it's nothing more than a smile-shaped scar, which will fade away more with time."

Jessica relaxed her neck. All her muscles appeared to have cramped up again. She'd need another massage if she went through with this. But maybe it was better to do this together with Liz, who didn't seem squeamish about looking at her scar. Jessica had even asked her a pretty unfair question and Liz had barely batted an eyelid. She needed someone as strong as Liz by her side to get through this.

Jessica nodded.

"I'll get that hand mirror I saw in the bathroom. I'll be right back."

Jessica followed Liz with her gaze. She was only wearing panties. If Jessica hadn't stopped them, they might be doing much more pleasant things right about now. But how could she even think of that as long as she hadn't seen herself?

Even though she was nervous, Jessica couldn't suppress a smile forming on her lips when Liz exited the bathroom.

"What?" Liz asked, obvious glee in her voice.

"I'm not sure I've ever seen a more beautiful woman in my life." Jessica chuckled to make herself sound a tad less serious, even though she meant every word. "You should be on television."

Liz chuckled with her. "Have I told you I don't have a TV? No Netflix subscription. Nothing. I don't watch television. What would I be doing *on* it?"

Jessica's eyes grew wide. "So you have more time for T-Rex." She gave Liz another once-over, more to stall than anything else. "It really works wonders for you."

Liz giggled. "It's called TRX. Total Resistance Exercise." She hopped onto the bed and put a hand on Jessica's belly again. "Are you ready for this?"

"I'm still flummoxed by your admission that you don't watch any television," Jessica said.

"We can talk about that later all you want," Liz said. She

put the mirror down. "How about you come and lie in my arms and I'll hold the mirror in front of us?"

Jessica inhaled deeply, then let the air flow from her mouth slowly. "Okay."

Liz sat up a bit and opened her arms wide.

Jessica pushed herself up. It was strange to not have any form of top on, not even a towel to protect her chest from view. She lay down in Liz's arms. Her breasts pushed against Jessica's back.

Before reaching for the mirror, Liz wrapped her arms around Jessica and pressed her lips to her cheek. No more words were needed right now.

She held Jessica until Jessica nodded and glanced at the mirror lying next to them.

Liz reached for it and brought it in front of them.

She held it up to their faces first. In the reflection, she blew Jessica an air kiss. Then she slowly started lowering the mirror. Their faces disappeared from view and Jessica closed her eyes, the way she had become accustomed to when standing in front of a mirror.

"Ready when you are," Liz said.

Jessica inhaled, then tried to relax into Liz's body. She opened one eye. The other one opened a sliver regardless of her trying to keep it shut. It made no difference if she looked with one or two eyes, anyway. One blind eye couldn't hide what she didn't want to see. Not if she dared to look in the mirror.

She blinked her eyes open properly. She looked above the mirror first, then let her gaze descend. She focused on her left breast, which, for a woman her age, she had always thought, looked very respectable. Then she finally took in the entire picture. The void on the right. The nothingness, broken only by a dark red scar curving upward.

Her throat tightened. Her breast was really gone. She

had felt it, this strange emptiness where before there had always been something. She had known every time she padded her right bra cup with a prosthesis when dressing. She had known even more so when she hadn't dared to look. But now she *was* looking. The scar didn't remind Jessica of a smile at all. Or perhaps it did look a little like one of those scary clown smiles. A blotch of red on a white surface. Something that wasn't supposed to be there. Something disconcerting no matter which way you looked at it.

She brought her hand to just underneath the scar tissue. Let it rest there for a moment. Then she ran a finger over the flatness of her chest, avoiding the scar at first.

All the while, Liz cradled Jessica with her strong arms, and held the mirror perfectly still.

Jessica's finger crept upward. She ran a fingertip over the outer edge of the scar. It was strangely smooth, but it wasn't the same smoothness as soft skin—of Liz's skin she had touched earlier. The texture was different, ridged in places, and as though it was coated with another kind of protective layer, a film of something she wasn't used to.

This had replaced her breast. It would have to do, at least for now. She could have reconstructive surgery later. Another operation. More scars. They could tattoo on a nipple. Jessica wasn't sure she wanted anyone to wield a scalpel on her body ever again—as long as her life didn't depend on it.

"I've seen enough," she said. "For now," she quickly added because she felt she should.

Liz put the mirror on the bed. "Anytime you need me to hold that mirror, I'll be there."

Jessica ignored the make-believe aspect of Liz's statement. In fact, Liz would be leaving soon. Jessica couldn't bear the thought of that.

She relaxed into Liz's arms. She didn't want to look at

her gorgeous face, nor see her perfect breasts, not for a little while.

Liz wrapped her arms around Jessica again. What they had just done together was, in many ways, much more intimate than having sex. How could Liz possibly go now?

"How are you feeling?" she whispered in Jessica's ear.

"Not very horny." Jessica chuckled. "Which is a damn shame now that I've got you almost naked in my bed."

"The night is young." Liz kissed her lightly on the cheek again. "How about I make us some dinner?"

Jessica huffed out some air. If this wasn't *the girlfriend experience*, she didn't know what was. A walk. A cup of coffee. A massage. And now dinner? All in one day.

Jessica freed herself from Liz's embrace. She looked around for the towel and wrapped it around her chest, then sat in front of Liz on her knees. "Quite honestly, I would love for you to stay a while longer, but I haven't just slipped into a different dimension. I haven't forgotten what this is. I know that what I want is not possible."

"Everything's possible," Liz said with a smile that totally belonged on television.

Jessica tilted her head. "I think we both know that's not true."

"After what just happened, I'm not just going to go, Jess." Liz reached out her hand and put it on Jessica's knee.

"I appreciate that." Jessica put a hand over Liz's. "But—"

"But what?" Liz squeezed Jessica's knee. "I'll stay as long as you want me to."

Jessica knitted her brows together. "Then I'd like—" Just in time, before she said anything too outrageous, she swallowed her words.

"Tell me." Liz scooted closer. "Tell me what you want."

Jessica waved off her question. "Never mind."

Liz pushed herself up. She mirrored Jessica's position and sat in front of her on her knees. "May I hazard a guess?" She took Jessica's hands in hers.

Jessica couldn't help but stare at Liz's chest. By the time she found the resolve to look up again, she could only say, "Yes."

"I think…" Liz caressed Jessica's palm with her thumb. "You'd like me to stay through the night."

Jessica scoffed.

Liz looked her in the eye. "Did I read that so wrong?"

"You're not a social worker, Liz. I'm very much aware of that."

"I'm not, but that step you just took… I'm not immune to that. It was a big thing. I want to stay. Of course, I won't if you don't want me to."

"You're so different than what I'm used to with Laurel," Jessica said.

"Your entire situation with Laurel was very different." Liz scooted closer on her knees. "Let's be clear, I'm not going to look you in the eye and tell you that I want to stay, solely out of the goodness of my heart. That would be wrong. But I feel things, too. And my gut is telling me to stay."

Jessica grimaced. "I'm glad we cleared that up."

"Let's just start with dinner, shall we?" Liz brought a finger to Jessica's chin.

Jessica looked into her bright smile. Every fiber of her being wanted to say yes to dinner with Liz.

"I'll do the cooking, remember?" Liz's smile transformed into a cocky grin.

"Does that mean you have to get dressed?"

"I can do 'naked chef'. I guess it'll depend on the ingredients I'm cooking with."

"I had a big shopping delivery this morning. There should be something you can work with."

"Great." Liz touched her palm to Jessica's cheek. "What would you normally do for dinner? Do you cook?"

"Sometimes. I used to enjoy cooking because it relaxes me. But, er…" Christ, this was going to make her sound like a spoiled rich girl again. "Well, my father's chef prepares a lot of my food. I have a freezer full of meals made by him. In fact, since my diagnosis, I haven't had a free spot in my freezer. My father even suggested I get an extra one to store all the food he's had prepared for me."

"That's so sweet."

"Maybe in some way." Jessica waved it off. "Let's not talk about my father."

Liz nodded. "So you don't actually need me to cook. I could just grab something from the freezer and pop it in the microwave."

"I'll just have to trust your integrity. And the smells coming from the kitchen."

"Hey, if anything, I'm a hooker with integrity." Liz laughed heartily.

Jessica shook her head. She took Liz's hand in hers and planted a kiss on her palm.

Chapter Eleven

"I HAD an advertising agency for ten years," Jessica said. She looked up from her plate, which contained a bunch of ingredients she didn't even know she had. Pomegranate seeds? She knew they were very trendy these days, but she had no idea how they had appeared on her shopping list. Although it wouldn't take a lot of sleuthing to find out who had decided Jessica needed pomegranate seeds in her diet. It was probably her stepmother, who loved a fad more than anything else. Jessica stuck her fork into a piece of tuna. "This is delicious by the way. Are you a chef as well as an art historian?"

"Okay. Hold up, please." Liz put her cutlery down. "I want to hear more about the advertising agency, but first I'd like to say I'm glad to hear you're enjoying the food. And no, I'm not a chef. I just really like a colorful plate of food. I always go by color when I cook. It must be the art buff in me."

Because of the delightful meal in front of her and Liz's left-field answers to her questions, Jessica was reminded of Katherine's words of the other day again. But for now, she decided to just enjoy the rest of the evening. If she had to break all ties with

Liz as of tomorrow, to protect her own heart, so be it. She still had tonight. She'd make the most of it—something she hadn't done in a good long while. "Do you follow the art world?" Jessica asked, well aware she was steering the conversation in a different direction again. A few minutes ago she'd been willing to talk about her failed business but now Liz was looking all too spectacular again, and was saying the kind of things that on any real date would have Jessica swooning, and Jessica couldn't bear to revisit her failures in front of this woman any longer.

"I collect a little." Liz's eyes lit up. "In my line of work, I get an interesting tip from time to time. A way in behind the scenes of certain galleries. There are many perks." She held Jessica's gaze. "Many," she repeated.

Jessica took a deep breath. She feared a dizzy spell if Liz kept talking like this—and looking in her eyes like that. "Picked up anything interesting lately?" She managed to squeeze the words past the constriction in her throat.

Liz arched up her eyebrows. "I might have." She folded her features into a more serious expression quickly, as though suddenly aware of crossing a boundary. "But let's get back to you. Tell me about your business." She reached for her glass of pinot noir—she had picked the wine as well. Jessica had, literally, only had to show up at her own dinner table. She'd certainly never had the all-inclusive service like the one Liz was offering now.

Jessica responded with a small shake of her head. "You're much more interesting to talk about."

"I assure you that I'm not." Liz leaned away from Jessica. "And you brought it up, which means you want to talk about it. I'm all ears. In fact, I'm rather curious."

Jessica sighed. "It was one big fiasco."

"So you keep saying, but give me some details, please?"

Jessica put down her fork. Her palms had gotten sweaty.

She rubbed them on the napkin in her lap. "It's hard to talk about."

"Surely it's not harder than what you did earlier?" Liz cocked her head.

Jessica leaned over the table. "You know, Liz, there's just something about you that doesn't quite gel with the reason you're here. It's quite disconcerting. It's making me quite unsure how to behave."

Liz nodded slowly. "I'm sorry about that. This is just how I am. I get that Laurel was different but there isn't some sort of standardized procedure to what we do. And in case you're wondering, I'm genuinely interested in you."

"That's what's so unnerving," Jessica said.

Liz stared at her for a few more seconds, then looked around the room. "Hold on." She walked toward a chair by the wall where her bag stood. She fished out her phone and fiddled with it for a bit. She headed back to the table and showed Jessica the screen. "I sent this message to the agency when I came down earlier. Before I started cooking. This means I'm off the clock."

Jessica glared at the message. It was just one word. A cold, sterile one-word sentence. *Done.*

"What does that mean?" Jessica asked.

Liz put her phone on the sideboard behind the table and took her seat across from Jessica again. "It means that, after you were so brave to look at yourself in the mirror for the first time since your surgery, I wanted to stay with you in a different capacity than the one I arrived in."

Jessica scoffed. "And what capacity might that be?"

Liz sucked her bottom lip into her mouth, as though she was giving this some serious thought. "Interested acquaintance, perhaps?" she said after a while.

"I'm still none the wiser." Jessica knew she was massively

on the defensive, but she wanted to make absolutely sure she wasn't misunderstanding anything.

"Okay, it looks like I'm going to have to spell this out for you." She slanted over the table. "I like you, Jessica Porter. I like spending time with you. I didn't much feel like going home. I think we had a bit of a moment earlier and I felt like exploring that more… in a *different capacity*."

Christ. Jessica didn't quite know how to react to that. She wanted to jump up, push Liz's chair back and shower her in all the affection she had saved up since her diagnosis, but something was holding her back. Caution. A gut feeling that something didn't quite add up. "Isn't that terribly unprofessional?" she asked.

Liz smiled. "Maybe," she said.

"I don't really know what to do with that." To prove her point, Jessica sipped from her glass of wine. She couldn't do much else. Her brain couldn't quite compute what was being said. She was afraid of misinterpreting what Liz was saying. In fact, she was sure she was hearing it all wrong.

"I'm sorry, Jess." Liz straightened her posture. "I shouldn't flirt like that. It's unfair."

"It's confusing." Jessica planted her elbows on the table. "To put it bluntly, I paid you to come here. That's what you do. That's the service I asked for. You came. We spent time together. But instead of leaving after my time with you was up, you decided to stay."

"That sounds about right." Liz pulled the sides of her blouse tightly over her chest. "But maybe I should go now." She rose. "I feel like the evening has taken a turn and that I perhaps got the wrong impression. I apologize for that."

The sight of Liz getting up tightened something in Jessica's stomach. "No, please don't leave." Jessica pushed her chair back. "I could use… an *interested acquaintance* right about now."

This brought a small smile to Liz's face. She walked over to where Jessica was sitting and squatted down next to her. "I feel like, under different circumstances, you and I could be friends, Jess." She glanced at her watch. "It's only eight o'clock. Maybe we can create some of those different circumstances tonight."

Jessica scrunched her lips together. "Friends, huh."

"Is that a problem?" Liz asked.

"Well, I have many friends, but I wouldn't dream of doing with them the things I'd like to do with you…"

"Something a bit different than friends then." Liz put her hands on Jessica's knees and pushed herself up. Once up, she brought her hands to the back of Jessica's chair and hovered over her. "Friends who enjoy doing this." She planted a kiss on Jessica's cheek. "Perhaps even this." The next kiss landed on Jessica's lips. "Or this." The next time Liz kissed Jessica, she opened her mouth and licked Jessica's lips with the tip of her tongue. Jessica didn't hesitate. She met Liz's tongue with hers and melted into their kiss.

When they broke apart, Jessica stared up at Liz's triumphant smile. "You seduced me."

"Who's to say it didn't happen the other way around?" Liz said.

Jessica loved Liz's quick wit. The way she had a response at the ready for anything Jessica said. And she adored that smile that, every time it was aimed at Jessica, truly did make her feel as though everything was going to be all right—just as Liz had promised her earlier that evening.

"I am," Jessica said. "And there's no doubt about it." She curved her arms around Liz's neck and pulled her closer so she could kiss her again.

Liz brought her long legs to either side of the chair and straddled Jessica. This time, she didn't hold back. She pushed her chest against Jessica's torso and let her tongue dance freely in her mouth.

"Would you like to go back upstairs?" Liz asked when they came up for air.

"Not yet," Jessica said.

Liz grinned at her. "That's right, you haven't told me about your business yet. Great way to get out of that." She pecked Jessica on the nose.

"I'm still processing what just happened," Jessica said.

Liz stood up from Jessica's lap and pulled a chair close. She took Jessica's hands gently in hers and nodded. "I can imagine it's a bit of a mind fuck."

"You're one big mind fuck. You being here is just… I don't know." Jessica didn't have the words to describe this highly unusual situation.

"How about this." Liz looked at their hands. "You take all the time you need to process but, in the meanwhile, we arrange a proper date." She locked her gaze on Jessica's. "One where you don't pay me at the end of the night."

"It would still be a mind fuck, but I do like the sound of that." She squeezed Liz's hand.

"It's a date then." Liz beamed, giving her a wide smile.

"Does that mean you're leaving now?" Jessica asked.

"Not if you want me to stay." Liz turned her gaze away and stared into the lounge. "How about you show me what's so exciting about watching television. I couldn't help but notice that monstrosity hanging from your wall. Why waste such prime space on a flat screen when you could hang a gorgeous piece of art instead?"

"Art is only entertaining for a few seconds. TV can keep me on the edge of my seat for hours." Jessica thought about how she'd felt about television that very morning. But it had been a long day. And she had a point to prove.

"Oh, the blasphemy." Liz clutched a hand to her chest.

"Art may require you to use a bit more of your imagination, sure, but doesn't that make it more rewarding?"

"More rewarding than an episode of *The Kramers*?" Jessica said. "I think not." She got up and held out her hand to Liz. "Come on, Miss High Brow, it's about time I corrupted you."

Chapter Twelve

LIZ HAD BEEN SHAKING her head for the past five minutes.

"Please, don't hold back on my account," Jessica said.

"I'm perplexed," Liz said. "And I cannot help but wonder what this sort of TV show being so popular says about our society as a whole."

"Oh, so now you want to have a discussion about the effect of *The Kramers* on society?" Jessica grinned.

"All that woman goes on about is how one particular brand of makeup is better than the other. I fail to see the entertainment value in this."

Jessica turned away from the screen. "This has to be one of the strangest days of my life."

"Why? Because it suddenly dawned on you that the company you work for produced this and it has instigated a deep crisis of faith in the TV industry?"

"Hey, you're the one who wanted to watch television."

"Nu-uh." Liz shook her head. "I'm the one who wanted to do very different things." She let her tongue flash over her upper lip.

"What I actually meant to say"—Jessica rolled her eyes

while, really, she couldn't believe how utterly comfortable she felt in Liz's company—"is that watching *The Kramers* with you was not what I thought I would be doing tonight. And I certainly didn't think you'd be all snooty about it."

"But tell me honestly, Jess. How else can one be about this but snooty? It's utter drivel. It makes me happy I don't have a television. In fact, it makes me never want to have one in my life." Liz had a smug smile on her face.

Jessica reached for the remote and switched off the television. "Better?" she asked.

"Much." Liz turned to her and drew her legs onto the couch.

Jessica sunk her teeth into her bottom lip and looked at Liz.

"Pressing matter on your mind?" Liz asked.

Jessica nodded.

"Does it have anything to do with Kathy Kramer? Because I can't help you with that."

"Is Liz your real name?" Jessica asked.

Liz didn't say anything for a few seconds. "It's Nicole Elizabeth Griffith. I never liked Nicole or even Nikki. I've always gone by my middle name. But my name on any official piece of paper would be Nicole Griffith."

"Nicole." Jessica regarded Liz intently. "You really don't strike me as a Nicole."

"That's what I told my mother years ago. Even she called me Liz, notwithstanding the occasional slip-up out of habit."

"Liz is much more glamorous," Jessica said.

"I know. It slips off the tongue so sensually." She chuckled.

"So you don't go by a fake name for, er, work purposes?"

"Nope."

"Is that… safe?"

"Perfectly so." Liz shuffled in her seat. "Look, Jess, the

clients I see are… how to put this. Me knowing their real name, which is something the agency demands, can be much more of an issue for them than them knowing *my* real name. Some girls use a fake name, but I don't like all that fake stuff. I like to provide an authentic experience." She drew her lips into a smile.

"You've certainly got the hang of that."

"But this is really me, Jess."

"Then what's the difference between you at this very moment and you when you're with a client? Say, you about two hours ago?"

"There really isn't much. I like being me. And sometimes I have to make things sound a little more exciting than they are, or I have to smile when I don't much feel like it, but I generally try to avoid those kind of situations."

"You make it sound so… easy."

"I provide a service that many people have the wrong idea about. Do I sleep with other women for money? Yes, that most certainly happens. But you know what? It doesn't even happen all of the time. Often, I'm someone's plus one. Women of a certain age really hate going to functions on their own. A lot of the time, I spend a few hours with someone just to brighten up their day."

"Like with me?" Jessica asked.

"Exactly."

"So, it's not weird that we… haven't done anything?"

Liz shook her head. "Of course not, although what happened today was highly unusual. We were definitely intimately involved. Much more so than if we'd had actual sex." She reached out her hand and touched Jessica's thigh. "'Weird' is really not a word that should come up."

"Well, Nicole," Jessica said, "I'll have to take your word for that." She snickered.

Liz shook her head again, but much more forcefully this

time. "If you start calling me Nicole, I can't be held responsible for the consequences." Her hand snuck up from Jessica's thigh to her belly, where she pinched her in the side.

"Ouch," Jessica squealed. "Have some respect for a cancer survivor's body, will you?"

Liz withdrew her hand and found her gaze. "I think someone just made a huge leap forward."

"How do you mean?"

"You just made a very lame cancer joke." Liz drew up her brow.

"Lame? How very dare you." Jessica mimicked Liz's earlier hand motion and pinched her in the side.

Liz held up her arms. "I surrender," she said in a dramatic voice. "Have mercy."

Jessica retracted her hand and glanced at Liz, who sat there with a wide grin plastered on her lips. "You know what would be a massive ratings hit?" Jessica straightened her posture. "*The Nicole Elizabeth Griffith Show*." She witnessed Liz's grin evaporate. "That smile. The wit. The wisdom. The intriguing life you lead."

"Oh sure, I can hear the voice-over already. Liz is about to visit a high-profile client. Jessica Porter really needs a seeing to today, so it would appear."

"I concede," Jessica said. "The format is dead in the water already." She snuck another glance at Liz, then looked away. She couldn't remember the last time she'd had so much fun.

Chapter Thirteen

"EARTH TO JESSICA. EARTH TO JESSICA," Caitlin said while she waved her fork in the air. "Are you so preoccupied with work already? You've only just come back."

Jessica had invited Caitlin to lunch after her second half day back at ANBC. She hadn't fared much better than the day before—and she was doubly distracted by the prospect of her date with Liz that evening.

"It's not work," Jessica said, surprising herself with the amount of glee in her voice. "I have a date tonight."

Caitlin's eyes grew wide. "A date?" She put down her fork. "How did you swing that?"

"What do you mean *how*? Some might consider me a most eligible bachelorette."

"Oh, I don't doubt it, Ms. Porter, but you haven't exactly been busy in any social circles now, have you? I'm just wondering where you met this dateable woman." Caitlin leaned back in her chair.

"She's a friend of a friend." Jessica wasn't going to tell Caitlin how she'd met Liz. "And I really, really like her."

Memories of last night flooded her mind again. They'd sat in the couch for a while longer, chatting and chuckling, until Jessica had gotten visibly tired and Liz had left. She'd kissed Jessica chastely on the cheek and had invited her to her place for their date the next day.

Jessica couldn't believe she was actually going to Liz's home tonight. She glanced at her watch. Only six more hours of unbearable anticipation to get through.

"Very mysterious," Caitlin said. "Is the friend anyone I know?"

"I'll tell you all about it later, okay? I shouldn't have brought it up. I'm probably massively jinxing it just by talking about it."

"Sure. Let's meet here again tomorrow so you can give me all the details." Caitlin flashed a smile.

"I'm a little nervous," Jessica said. "It's been a while since I last went on a proper date."

"If it's meant to be, it'll work out."

"It's… rather complicated…" Jessica waved off her own statement. "But no need to get into that now." While she was excited about seeing Liz again, and it had, indeed, been ages since she'd gone on a date, it was hard to ignore Liz's profession and its ramifications. When it all came down to it, Jessica should know better than to fall for a call girl. "How's your show going?"

"Do you mean to say you haven't been watching?" Caitlin asked, her tone mock-serious.

"Of course I have. I never miss an episode of *The Caitlin James Show*. How could I? Best hour of my week." Jessica shot Caitlin a grin.

"Then you will know we're doing fine. No complaints. Production-wise, it's like a well-oiled machine by now. Thank goodness we have a wide variety of guests who can keep things interesting. Speaking of, as much as I love having my compatriots on the show, I've been working on a more international wish list. I may need your connections if I want to make some of it come true."

"If by that you mean my father's connections, I'm not sure I can help," Jessica said on a sigh.

Caitlin narrowed her eyes and regarded Jessica intently. "Where's that annoying enthusiasm you hit me over the head with after you just started this job, Jess? Remember the good old days when you made me interview Kathy Kramer? I did that for you. I'm just cashing in my favor, that's all."

"I think that enthusiasm was cut out of me along with the cancer." She let her hands fall into her lap. "I can't seem to muster much of it for anything job-related these days."

Caitlin pursed her lips together for a brief moment before she said, "Did you come back to work too early? There's no shame in that. You only took three months off and what you went through was so life-changing."

"I want to work. I want to do something. It's just this job… I don't know. The thought of jumping back in hasn't exactly lit me up."

"I guess that's to be expected. I would just give it some time. Work half days for a while. Get your head back into the game. Go on a few dates. Pick your life back up again."

"That's the thing. I'm not so sure there's that much of my pre-cancer life I want to pick back up. This job…" She shrugged. "I'm grateful for the chance my father gave me after my business went under, but it's not like I had many choices back then. Not if I wanted to work. I think a lot of my enthusiasm from back then was due to the simple fact that I was able to work again after I… crawled out of depression. The energy that came with that just propelled me forward. I don't seem to have that same kind of energy right now. If anything, I feel much more like when I was still suffering from depression. Like this numbness is hanging over me." *Except last night when I was giggling with Liz.*

"Have you been seeing…" Caitlin tapped a finger on the table. "What's her name again?"

"Mrs. Buchman," Jessica said. "No. I haven't seen her for a while. I don't feel like seeing her. I don't feel like rehashing all my emotions concerning cancer again. I just want to stop thinking about it and get on with my life, but I can't seem to be able to."

Caitlin leaned over the table. "I wish I could help you."

"You have helped." There was that tremor in Jessica's voice again—she never used to have that before her surgery. It was as though having cancer had pushed her feelings to a place inside her from where they could well up at the most inopportune moments. "You're helping now by being here," Jessica managed to say. "By listening to me."

"I wish I could do more." Caitlin reached out her hand over the table.

Jessica accepted the display of affection and grabbed hold of Caitlin's fingers. "I thought I could face it alone. That's why I pulled that disappearing act." She shook her head. "I was so wrong."

"The point is that you're not alone." Caitlin squeezed back. "You have me and Jo. You have Katherine. You have your family. You have your friend who introduced you to a woman you're going on a date with."

Jessica nodded. She'd just been starting to find her feet again after her depression when she'd gotten the cancer diagnosis. Even though the surgery had been successful, and Jessica had a good prognosis for full remission, she felt like she had taken too many steps backward. As though the healing of one disease had undone some of the healing of the previous one.

"Her name's Liz." Jessica held up a finger of her free hand. "But you can't tell anyone about this, okay?"

"My lips are sealed. The name Liz is locked up inside of me." Caitlin turned on her TV smile. It was infectious and Jessica couldn't help but mirror it—or maybe it was just the mention of Liz's name.

"Quite frankly, she's the most gorgeous woman I've ever laid eyes on." Jessica felt herself go soft inside. She let go of Caitlin's hand and leaned back, allowing images of Liz to fill her mind. "But it's not just that. She's so easy to be around. We really hit it off the other night. She… pushed me in all the right ways. And now I can't stop thinking about her."

"That's a lot of information," Caitlin said. "I need a few moments to process." She stared at Jessica as though trying to read more information off her face. "So you've spent significant time with this woman already?"

Jessica nodded.

"But you're not going to tell me about it?"

"I can't. It's… delicate."

Caitlin's eyes grew wide. "*Delicate?* Is she married? Famous and in the closet? Part of the upper echelons of society?" She chuckled.

"None of that."

"Come on, Jess. You'll have to give me something. The suspense is killing me." Caitlin brought a hand to her throat and pretended to suffocate.

"I want to tell you. God, I do. But you have to promise me that you won't judge."

Caitlin cocked her head. "Do you even know me?" She waved her hand theatrically. "Yoohoo, it's me, Caitlin James! Rattler of the bourgeoisie mind. Upsetter of many a traditional thinker."

"Even so." Jessica's voice had gone down a notch. "I still think you might judge."

"Only one way to find out." Caitlin fixed her gaze on Jessica.

"Liz is… a friend of Katherine's." She looked Caitlin in the eye. "And by friend, I mean colleague."

"I see." Caitlin slowly nodded. "Just for the record, I'm not judging. I'm just processing the facts."

"Take your time," Jessica said. "I sure as hell haven't processed them yet."

"So Katherine introduced you to her colleague and you hit it off?" Caitlin asked. She wasn't born yesterday. Someone like Caitlin would put two and two together quickly.

"I, um, booked Liz's services." Jessica chuckled nervously. "Nothing happened. We just talked and walked around. Had dinner." She paused. "Well, then I booked her again and showed her my scar."

"Still not judging, but I must admit I'm a little surprised."

"Anyway, how I met her is beside the point. The fact is that I met her and that I like her and I think she likes me too, but of course Katherine thinks I'm crazy. I can't talk to her about this."

"I have to ask this. I wouldn't be a good friend if I didn't." Caitlin looked away for a moment. "You don't think Liz is leading you on?"

"No," Jessica said curtly.

"Okay," Caitlin replied.

"I know how this sounds," Jessica said. "Like I've lost my mind after my surgery." Jessica shook her head. "Even *I* thought I had for a minute. But I haven't. Honestly, Caitlin, you should meet her, then you'd understand."

"I'd love to. Bring her to dinner next weekend."

"Let's not get too ahead of ourselves. I need to see how the date goes first," Jessica said, even though the prospect appealed to her very much.

"Of course. I just don't want you to think that Liz is not welcome at ours."

"I'd never think that. You invited Katherine, remember?"

"Bring Liz. You've got me all curious now," Caitlin said.

"If I bring Liz, I'll have to tell Katherine first." Jessica rested her chin on her upturned palms. "It's not going to go down well."

"Don't tell her. Just show up." Caitlin grinned.

"All that drama in your gorgeous penthouse." Jessica chuckled.

"Drama and a view, what's better than that?" Caitlin quipped.

"I'll let you know," Jessica said.

"I'm here for you, Jess. You can talk to me about anything, and that includes Liz." She glanced at Jessica with a funny look in her eyes. "But... how do you feel about Liz's profession?"

"Isn't that the million-dollar question," Jessica said. "I have rather complicated feelings toward it. And I'm not so naive to think it won't stand in the way of a straightforward romance." She shook her head. "Even though I really shouldn't be using the word romance. It's just a date."

"It's more than a date. I can tell by the way you talk about her."

"I haven't felt like this in such a long time, but, you know, I can never be quite sure it isn't the cancer talking. Why am I feeling like this? Because she was so kind to me? Because I was blinded by her beauty? Is it all even real?" Jessica sighed. "I really don't know."

"Time will tell. And if there's one thing you can always count on it's for time to pass."

"Thanks." Jessica looked at her friend. "One good thing has come from me taking this job at ANBC. Meeting you.

I'm serious. And I'm allowed to be corny because, well, you know…"

"If only you'd been this corny when we first met." Caitlin sent her a big smile.

Jessica glanced at her as warmth spread through her chest.

Chapter Fourteen

Jessica had dressed casually for the date. They weren't going to a fancy restaurant, after all. She showed up at Liz's door at her Bondi Beach address, in a beige pair of trousers and a navy shirt on top. She'd brought two bottles of Pinot Noir. She rang the bell and, for a split second, wondered if the people living across the hall knew what Liz did for a living. Jessica pushed the thought away and then the door swung open.

"Hello, hello." Liz gave her a big smile. "Welcome to my humble abode." She threw her arms wide for Jessica to step into.

It was an awkward hug because Jessica was holding the bag with the bottles of wine and, even more so, the familiarity with which they had left things the previous night wasn't there yet. It couldn't possibly be.

"Sit. Make yourself comfortable," Liz said. Her voice sounded a little different—as though she too was a little nervous.

Jessica looked around Liz's living room. The last of the light outside slanted in through big windows.

Liz took the bottles of wine from the bag Jessica had handed her and examined the labels. "We'll be having excellent red tonight then." She put one bottle on the dining table and brought the other one into the sitting area.

"What a lovely place," Jessica said. Totally different from Katherine's home, she thought. But she really should stop comparing Liz to Katherine—or Laurel. People in the same profession didn't live carbon copies of each other's lives. "Do you own it?"

"No." Liz carried over two wine glasses. "I'm not really one for owning property. I like the freedom that comes with renting."

"And the sky-high Sydney rent?"

Liz waved her arm around. "The square footage of this place isn't huge. And I get by." She winked at Jessica. "My landlady is very nice, actually."

Something tightened in Jessica's stomach. What did that mean? That Liz paid rent with other means than just money? She pushed the thought out of her mind. She couldn't spend the evening with ideas like that swarming around in her head.

Jessica sat down. "Your decor is very Scandi-chic," she said.

"Is it?" Liz looked around her living room as though reassessing it. "If by that you mean most of my furniture is from Ikea, you're half right." She chuckled.

Liz poured them a glass of wine and handed one to Jessica. She looked into her eyes as she did. "I'm glad you're here," she said.

"Me too." One gaze into Liz's eyes and Jessica was ready to forget most thoughts she had walked in here with. "I didn't mean to imply that your furniture is from Ikea. I actually meant—"

Liz silenced her with a grin. "It's fine. I'm not sensitive

about my furniture." She sat next to Jessica and drew one knee up onto the couch so that it touched the side of Jessica's thigh. "Let me try this wine you brought." She made a performance of pushing her nose into the glass, taking a sip and swirling the wine around in her mouth. "All I can say is that it's exquisite, Ms. Porter," she exclaimed. "You have great taste."

"So do you." Jessica noticed the Xiao Mei Chong on the wall across from where she was sitting. "How long have you had that?"

"Almost ten years." Liz gazed at the painting as well. "Bought it for less than two grand."

Jessica's eyes grew wide. "Wow. It must be worth several times that now." She looked at Liz. "Do you have any other gems like that?"

"I'll give you a tour later." She grinned at Jessica. Clearly Liz's mind was not on art. "If only I had more wall space."

"Feel free to hang any excess art at my house," Jessica blurted out before she realized how presumptuous that sounded.

Liz glanced at her in silence. "It's my dream to open an art gallery someday. After I've retired."

"Retired," Jessica repeated. "Do you have a set retirement age in your… business?"

Liz shook her head while she chuckled. "Not really. But most of my colleagues quit soon after forty."

"Is that your plan as well?" Jessica sipped from the wine. Excellent as it may be, she was too distracted waiting for Liz's reply to pay much attention to its taste.

"Yes. Although it depends. Starting an art gallery requires a fair bit of capital. Barring any unforeseen circumstances, I should have the money in a few years."

"Is it terribly indiscreet to ask how old you are?" Jessica

shuffled around. "You probably already know that I'm forty-five."

"I'm thirty-nine. It's not a secret. I've never understood why women are so coy about their age."

Jessica shrugged. "Just another thing pushed upon us by women's magazines."

"Doesn't your father own a few of the worst offenders?" Liz asked. "If you're sick of TV, maybe you can go into the women's magazines business and shake things up a little. You'd be doing many women a favor." Liz pushed a strand of dark hair behind her ear.

"Hm." Jessica bunched her lips together. "No, TV is higher on my work wish list than magazines, I'm afraid."

"How about going back to advertising?" Liz asked.

"I've thought about it, but my name isn't going to inspire a lot of confidence in possible clients after what happened." She took another sip of wine.

"Is this where you finally tell me about it?" Liz's voice was sweet. "Full disclosure. I tried to google it, but didn't find a thing."

"Never underestimate the reach of Edward Porter when it comes to keeping his reputation untarnished. And to be clear, that reputation extends to anything that could reflect badly on him, including his daughter's illness."

"You were ill?" Liz asked. Her knee still rested against Jessica's thigh.

"I suffered from the disease so many women my age suffer from. We try to do too much while also trying to prove that we're up for the job, which costs us double the effort as men because we need to first convince ourselves that we're not imposters. Then we have to convince all the people around us." She sighed. "Most days, I started work from home at 6 a.m., putting in a few hours before going to the office, and I didn't stop until midnight. It was pure madness when I look back on it. These days, I'm not sure what I was trying to prove. I'm pretty certain it didn't help with keeping my body cancer free."

"Oh, no, please don't blame yourself for that." There was a twinge of agitation in Liz's voice. "My mother used to say things like that as well. If only I hadn't done this or that —the list was endless. But it's so pointless."

Jessica shook her head. "You can't help it though."

Liz just nodded.

"I burned out completely. I sank into a deep depression. My managing skills took a nose dive. I lost us one big client, which was like the first in a line of very well-aligned dominos. The business went under in less than a year."

"I'm so sorry to hear that." Liz put a hand on Jessica's knee.

"Maybe it happened for a reason. Clearly, I couldn't go on the way I had been. I was ignoring all the warning signs." Jessica looked into her wine glass. "Of course, my father stepped in to take care of everything. He made sure my employees got handsome severance packages and he paid off my debtors. In theory, the business never officially folded, but in my head, it did." She looked up again. "He hasn't really treated me the same since." She pulled up one shoulder. "I guess I've always been a disappointment to him."

"Is it the classic story of you not wanting to take over his empire?" Liz's tone was free of judgment.

"In a way, but it's a bit more complicated than that." She leaned back into the couch. "But maybe we can keep that story for another time." She narrowed her eyes. "I want to know more about you."

"I have very few secrets," Liz said and threw her arms wide as if to illustrate her point.

"Really?" Jessica drew her lips into a skeptical pout. "I mean, I do hope you have some."

"Well, yes, professional discretion is paramount. That's a given."

"How did your parents react to you coming out?" Jessica asked.

Liz gave a small shrug. "Not much at all. It wasn't a shock nor a surprise. I guess they knew much sooner than I did. And my father is, well… he simply doesn't care about any of that. Maybe my mother was a bit worried about my future, but if she was, she didn't really show it. It was the most undramatic non-event. The way all coming-outs should be, really."

"*Should* be, yes. But not all parents are like yours, unfortunately," Jessica said on a sigh.

"Oh, that's—" Liz was interrupted by the loud ring of her phone. It lay vibrating wildly on the arm rest of the couch. She shot up and grabbed it to look at the screen. "I'm sorry, I really need to take this."

Jessica nodded.

Liz exited the living room and only took the call when she was in the other room and had closed the door behind her.

Jessica looked around the living room, but her attention focused on the sound of Liz's voice next door. It could be anyone calling her, but Jessica tried to think of whom of her friends or family she would allow to interrupt a date with a phone call. She concluded that, barring very few exceptions, she wouldn't pick up. Liz said she *had to* take this call. It pushed Jessica's thoughts in a direction she would rather steer clear of, but that was easier said than done.

"Sorry about that." Liz entered the living room again, all smiles. She put her phone on a bookshelf against the furthest wall. "I promise we won't be disturbed again." She sat down next to Jessica, but this time, left a little more space between their bodies so they didn't touch. "I believe you were about to tell me about your coming out?"

Jessica gained some time by drinking from her wine. "Can I ask you something instead of telling you my depressing coming out story?"

"Of course." Liz's smile was a bit tight, as though she already knew perfectly well what Jessica wanted to ask her.

"That call you just took… Was that the agency?"

Liz's smile grew even more thin-lipped. "It was."

Jessica tried to look into Liz's eyes but she couldn't. She had to look away.

"Is that a problem?" Liz asked.

"I honestly don't know," Jessica said. "I guess I have a bit of a problem with it, otherwise I wouldn't bring it up."

Liz shook her head. "It's normal for you to react this way, but I will tell you that I'm way past defending what I do for a living. I'm fine with what I do."

"Have you had, er, many relationships since you started?"

Liz chuckled. "No, not really. Because, guess what? Most women seem to have a really big problem with my profession. Me being so unapologetic about it doesn't help matters much."

Jessica didn't know what to say to that. She could hardly be holier than thou about it. She had met Liz because she had hired her. But Liz getting that call gave her a very different feeling—it made her feel that, even on their first real date, she already had to share Liz.

"Look." Liz shuffled a little closer. "Even though I will never apologize for what I do, I do understand it's difficult for other people to accept. This may be the so-called oldest profession in the world, but it comes with more preconceptions and judgement than anything else." Liz looked at Jessica's knee first before she put her hand back where it had been before she had received the call. "If you don't want this date to continue—and I'll understand if that's the case—there will be no hard feelings, I promise. Although I will be disappointed, of course." She cocked her head and shot Jessica a quick grin. "For the record, I like you a lot and I would very much like for it to continue." Her thumb pushed into Jessica's thigh. "We're going to need very clear communication from the beginning, which may take away a bit of the magic, but, let's be honest, I think we're going to have to bypass some of that either way simply because of how we met."

Jessica couldn't help herself. The warmth she'd felt when sitting in front of the TV with Liz the other day had remained inside her so vividly—because it contrasted so heavily with how she'd been feeling for months. She put her own hand over Liz's. "I like you more than a lot," she said. "And I totally agree about the very clear communication. Does that mean I can ask questions freely?"

"Yes, as long as you don't ask for details about my clients, because you know I can't give those."

Jessica nodded her understanding. "That phone call you just got," she asked, "was that to set up a date?"

"Yes." Liz drew her lips into a half pout.

Jessica took her time to absorb the information. "A regular?" she asked after a while.

"You could say that." Liz glanced around then reached for her glass on the coffee table, all the while keeping her hand beneath Jessica's.

"For when?"

"Friday evening."

"Do you often… work on weekends?"

Liz nodded. "Yes."

"How many dates do you go on in an average week?" Jessica was starting to feel like a journalist researching a long article about the subject.

"No one week is the same, but…" Liz paused to think. "Never more than three."

"Is that your own choice or something the agency imposes?"

"My own choice." A small smile was starting to form around Liz's lips.

"You said the woman you got the call about is a regular. Does that mean a weekly standing appointment?"

Liz shook her head. "No. That's not a service I provide."

"But if someone was to request you every week, you wouldn't say no?"

Liz chuckled. "If someone did that, it would cost them a hell of a lot of money."

"So? Money is no issue for these women, I presume."

"I think I get where you're going with this and we do have guidelines about this. Most of it we handle on instinct, and if I start to sense that a regular pattern is occurring for any other reason than the service I provide, then I take measures. I become unavailable for the client for a while. But this hardly ever happens. Yes, people are easy to fool in the short term, but long term is something else entirely. Most people know what they're buying—and it's not love, just temporary affection."

"Isn't it against some guideline for you to have invited me to your home for an actual date?"

"Not if you no longer book me." Liz drew up her eyebrows. "Is that going to be a problem?"

Jessica burst into a chuckle. "It shouldn't be, no."

"Good." Liz squeezed her knee. "I wouldn't take your money, anyway." She found Jessica's gaze and their eyes met.

Jessica tried to determine the color of Liz's eyes. They were lighter than most brown eyes she'd seen, but they also had specks of green in them.

"Enough with the twenty questions now?" Liz asked. "Are you hungry?"

"Sure." Jessica could do with a break from receiving all those candid answers. She needed some time to digest what she'd already learned. She wasn't hungry in the least, however.

"Let's eat." Liz didn't get up immediately. Her hand remained tucked underneath Jessica's for a few more seconds as they looked into each other eyes.

In her glance, Jessica saw much more than answers to the many questions she had. She was faced with feelings she perhaps shouldn't have—not if she wanted to keep her life simple while she was only just beginning to build it back up. But Liz was already a big part of the rebuilding of her existence, and what was fun about a simple life, anyway?

Chapter Fifteen

"My father was very disappointed when I came out. In the true sense of the word," Jessica said, when they'd nearly finished eating. "He wasn't angry or blaming himself or any of the other classic reactions. It was like something I was doing *to* him. By the time I could make him understand that this was how I was born, too much had been broken between us. And we weren't exactly close before."

"And your mother?" Liz asked.

"My mother. Gosh." Jessica huffed out some air. "By the time I came out, I hadn't seen my mother in ten years. I called her because, for some reason, I thought she should know. She sounded as if she didn't care much either way."

"That's a rough deal."

Jessica shrugged. "By then, I didn't care much what my mother thought of me. She and my father divorced when I was five. I stayed with my father. It wasn't my choice. I was never asked. It was just decided for me. But it was definitely the better choice. Anyone who has ever claimed that maternal instinct comes naturally to any woman who has given birth is very, very wrong. Some people are simply emotionally unfit to be parents. My mother is one of those people."

"Jesus, Jess." Liz put her fork down. "That sounds so horrible."

"It's fine. I didn't have a bad childhood. I had the most fabulous nanny. The same one until I turned thirteen. Her name was Emily. She raised me single-handedly. And guess what? She didn't take it as a personal affront at all when I told her I was a lesbian." Jessica put her cutlery down as well. "Parenting is so much more than being someone's mother or father. Emily was so much more of a parent to me than my real parents. I did have one stepmother once who took a bit of an interest, but that marriage didn't last very long and after a while you learn to not get attached to new people in your life too quickly."

"What happened after you turned thirteen? Why did Emily stop being your nanny?"

"My father decided I was becoming too much of a brat and sent me to boarding school."

"Is that where you became a lesbian?" Liz asked, her voice serious but her eyes filled with glee.

Jessica burst out laughing. "Of course. No cliché has gone unexplored in my poor little rich girl's life." She glanced at Liz from under her lashes. "Boarding school wasn't too bad. In fact, it was good for me. I was on many a sports team." She waggled her eyebrows. "It helps."

"I bet it does." Liz winked at her. "Do you still see Emily?"

"She passed away three years ago." Jessica's throat still constricted at the thought of Emily no longer being there.

"I'm so sorry to hear that." Liz sighed. She paused for a bit until she asked her next question. "Did you call your mother when you got your cancer diagnosis?"

Jessica shook her head. "I had no reason to. She wasn't

going to offer me much comfort, was she? And my father was already acting totally out of control. His only child having cancer and there was nothing his money could do about it. Another notch on the disappointment belt."

"Surely he wasn't disappointed because you fell ill."

"I'm pretty sure he was, although, this time, he didn't say as much. Not like when my company went bust or I came out. Or I wasn't born as a boy. Or at the very least wasn't a more respectable heir."

"Sounds like there's some bad blood there."

Jessica shrugged. "It's better now. He's been quite different, actually. He's pushing seventy-five. I guess that's an age that makes you think about things a little differently."

"Maybe. He's not thinking about retiring yet?"

"He'll die working. He'll never stop. Actually, I think it would be bad for him to stop. What would he do? He loves what he does now, so why stop?"

"I do agree. If you enjoy your work, why retire?"

"Does that mean you don't always enjoy your work? You *are* thinking of retiring?" Jessica didn't feel like talking about her family any longer.

"My case is different. Some jobs are not meant to be done for life. Imagine me dying on the job." Her lips formed into a smile, but it wasn't reflected in her eyes.

"That would be a tough one."

"Without wanting to romanticize my job, I do enjoy it. It's very sociable and I like to be around people. It puts me in touch with some very interesting characters. And I have much more sex than most."

"If you put it like that." Jessica took a quick drink.

"But just like any profession, there are down sides. No job is all plus sides. Life isn't like that. We all have to make compromises."

Jessica peered into her wine glass. Another pressing question had taken hold of her, but she didn't know how to ask it.

"Come on then," Liz said. "Out with it. I'm ready for a second round of twenty questions, although I would appreciate it if we could keep it to only ten this time." She pushed her plate a little farther on the table and leaned her elbows on the tabletop.

"It's a silly question, really."

"Did no one ever teach you that there's no such thing as a silly question?" Liz asked.

"No, I was raised on real talk and that's just bullshit. At least that's what my father would say."

"Well, I'm sure your question is perfectly valid. Come on. Let me have it."

"Okay." Jessica took her wine glass in her hands. It made her feel less vulnerable. "When you're with a client. In bed. Do you ever, er…"

"Yes?" Liz asked.

"You know. Come." A hot flush crept up Jessica's cheeks.

"Sure." Liz sent her a smile. "It really depends on the situation. Some women really get off on that. If the vibe between us is right, I do sometimes let go. Although mostly I do have to fake it. There are so many different scenarios. But it has happened, although it's definitely not part of my job description." Her smile widened. "Now can I ask you a question?"

"It would be pretty rude to say no at this point." Jessica mirrored Liz's smile.

"What happened when you had Laurel over? Did you insist on making her come?"

The previous blush had scarcely faded before Jessica's cheeks were again engulfed in hotness. "Well, er, I didn't insist," she stammered. "But I did try. Although I'll never know whether she faked it or not."

"Interesting." Liz sat there nodding as though she had just uncovered a hidden truth about Jessica.

"It's really not that interesting."

"Oh, it is." Under the table, Jessica felt Liz's shin slide against hers. "Can I interest you in some dessert? I make the lightest chocolate mousse you'll ever taste," she said.

"That's a bold claim to make." Jessica let her leg lean into Liz's. She was glad for the break in their conversation. Her cheeks needed some urgent cooling off.

"I've just realized I may have said that to the wrong person. Does your father have a pastry chef?"

"Nope. Edward Porter is not a dessert man."

"Well, then. Let's see if I can impress you."

"This was delicious, by the way." Jessica grabbed her plate and started to rise.

"No, no, no. Please remain seated. Or stretch your legs, if you like. But there's no need to help." Liz quickly rose, and took the plate from Jessica's hand. "The kitchen is a right old mess. I want you as far away from there as possible."

"Ah, that explains it." Jessica sat down again and leaned back in her chair. "I'll stay in the safe zone then."

"If you want to feel useful, you can always pour us some more wine," Liz said and disappeared into the kitchen.

Jessica refilled their glasses and rehashed all the things that had been said. No matter the oddity of the subjects, Liz was still so easy to talk to. She had so much confidence, she made up for what Jessica lacked right now.

"Has the person who invented the dishwasher ever received a Nobel Prize?" Liz sauntered back into the living room. "Because no greater service has ever been done to humankind." She carried two low glasses filled to the brim with chocolate mousse. "Here you go, Madam. Did you want coffee or tea with that?"

"Wine will be fine," Jessica said.

"Here's to a wonderful date." Liz picked up her wine glass.

Jessica joined her in the toast. It might be an unusual date, but that didn't make Jessica feel any less special when she was in Liz's company.

Chapter Sixteen

THEY WERE BACK on the couch, steadily working their way through the second bottle of wine. Jessica was contemplating calling in sick at work the next day. It was only her third day back, but no one would bat an eyelid if she did. Someone would probably tell her father—he had spies in all departments—and then she'd have to deal with him. She actually preferred him a bit more aloof than the worried persona he had adopted since she'd gotten sick.

"I can't believe I have to go to work tomorrow." Jessica heeled off her shoes and stretched her legs onto the ottoman. "You also made me eat too much. I need to lie down."

"Don't get too comfortable." Liz scooted next to her and stretched her legs as well. "I still need to give you a tour of the premises."

"Ah yes, your art collection. Maybe we can save it for next time. Yours will make mine look like child's play, anyway."

"Are you kidding? You have a Robert Barrow hanging in your hallway. Not even in the living room; in the hallway of all places."

"For that welcoming feeling."

"More like intimidating." Liz leaned into her.

"Only if you're in the know."

Jessica felt Liz nod next to her. "So," she said after a beat. "The hour is getting late and the lady is getting tired." She put a hand on Jessica's thigh. "Can I put you down for a second date or do you need to get back to me on that?"

"Is this your way of sending me home?" Jessica asked.

"Goodness, no." Liz turned to her. "You just look as though you might fall asleep any minute now."

Jessica sighed. "My stamina needs a little work. It has taken a bit of a hit lately." She tried to square her shoulders. "But it's just a post-dinner slump. I'll get a second wind in a bit."

"Pity we can't watch some of *The Kramers* to pass the time," Liz joked.

"Exactly what I was going to say." Jessica slid her hand underneath Liz's and intertwined their fingers. "Whatever will we do to make time go faster?"

"Seeing as this is, technically, our first date, our options are limited, I guess." Liz grinned.

"Although we have seen each other half naked," Jessica said.

"And we've kissed and watched television together," Liz replied.

Jessica's breath stalled in her throat. She was glad she and Liz had only kissed while Liz was on the clock, so to speak. Liz had shown her the message she had sent to the agency. It had sent a clear message to Jessica as well.

"I've introduced you to the wonderful world that is my job." Jessica rotated a little so she could see Liz's face better. "You do realize we're now living in a time dubbed *Peak TV*."

"Aren't we the lucky ones," Liz said.

Jessica snickered. "You can be so snobbish."

"Moi?" Liz put a hand to her chest. "With my Scandi-chic furniture?"

Jessica slapped her on the thigh. "Enough already. I was nervous when I first arrived. Have some mercy."

Liz leaned in a little closer and whispered, "Are you begging for mercy already?"

Jessica swiveled her head and looked Liz straight in the eye. She had a smile on her lips, but her eyes told a different story. Jessica wanted to bridge the few inches between their faces and feel Liz's lips on hers again, but something was holding her back. The exact same thing that had been holding her back for a long time. Fear.

"Too much, too soon?" Liz asked and squeezed Jessica's hand.

Jessica shook her head while she sank her teeth into her bottom lip.

"Good." Liz's voice had dropped an octave. She *did* have the guts to bridge the tiny distance between them and pressed her lips softly against Jessica's. She withdrew for a split second until their lips met again the next moment.

Liz slid her fingers from between Jessica's and brought her hand to Jessica's cheek. She touched the back of her fingers against the spot where Jessica had blushed so fever-ishly earlier. The touch made Jessica flush again, but she didn't care this time around. She pushed her cheek against Liz's hand while she pressed her lips against Liz's. It was the only logical outcome. Jessica wanted Liz. There had never been any doubt about that.

And Liz wanted Jessica too. That much was obvious by the way her tongue slipped between Jessica's lips, by the way her body twisted to meet as much of Jessica's as possible.

"Let me get a bit more comfortable," Liz said when they

came up for air. She pushed herself up and crawled onto Jessica's lap, planting her knees on either side of Jessica. "Hi," she said, when they were face-to-face again.

"Hi." Jessica's voice was hoarse and deep.

Liz kissed her again, palming Jessica's cheeks with both hands. The kiss was deep and impossible to misinterpret.

"I want you," Liz said, when they broke from the kiss. She was panting slightly and something had changed in her eyes again. She looked as though she had them firmly on the prize—there was no doubt the prize was Jessica.

"I want you too," Jessica managed to say.

Liz smiled at her. "Come," she said. She climbed off Jessica and held out her hand. "Let me show you my boudoir."

Jessica giggled as she extended her hand and let Liz pull her out of the couch. Liz slung an arm around her and held her tightly as she led Jessica into the bedroom. Jessica had no eyes at all for anything on the walls. She only felt Liz's arm around her and her own heart beating away in her chest.

"Welcome," Liz said, and closed the door behind them. They stood in complete darkness. "Oops, sorry about that." Liz let go and stumbled around. A few seconds later a lamp on the bedside table lit up the room. "Not as suave as I had hoped to be." Liz grabbed Jessica's hand again.

The sudden illumination drew Jessica's glance to the wall behind the lamp. A large black and white photo hung above Liz's bed, portraying a stark naked woman from the back. The woman flexed her muscles and boasted an impressive shoulder line. Jessica couldn't explain how, but even though she couldn't see her face, and wasn't that familiar with her naked shoulder line yet, she knew it was Liz.

"Is there a particular reason you have a naked picture of yourself hanging above your bed?" Jessica asked.

"There are many." Liz stood next to her and looked at the picture with Jessica. "The main one being this type of reaction." She put her hand in the small of Jessica's back. "How did you know it was me?"

"Something about it is just so quintessentially you."

"Ah, must be the impressive posterior chain." Liz let her hand drop and gently slapped Jessica's bottom.

"It's rather intimidating, actually. For women like me who are not exactly in their prime." Jessica pushed her behind into Liz's hand regardless.

"Believe it or not, but not many women make it into my boudoir," Liz said. "In fact, you're the first since I hung that up. I'm still kind of testing it out." Liz followed up with a chuckle.

"So you'll get me to fill in a survey later on the effects it had?" Jessica leaned against Liz's side. She felt so solid and strong.

"That's exactly right." Liz's hand sneaked up again and slid under the hem of Jessica's blouse.

"Who took that picture? It's hardly a candid shot."

"A friend of mine who dabbles in amateur photography."

"Impressive for an amateur."

Liz's fingertips traced a line up Jessica's spine. "Do you mean even more so than the subject of the picture?"

"God no." The hair on the back of Jessica's neck stood up. "Nothing's more impressive than that."

Liz slipped behind her and moved both her hands underneath Jessica's blouse, coming to rest on her belly. Her lips found Jessica's neck and traced a path up to her ear.

"I want you," Liz repeated her words from earlier in the living room. "So much." She withdrew her hands from Jessica's belly and she kissed her neck again, then started to unbutton her blouse. It was obviously a skill she had perfected because mere seconds later, Jessica's blouse slid off her shoulders.

Liz brought her hands to Jessica's hips and gestured for her to turn around. Jessica stood facing Liz in her bra, but she wasn't engulfed with the familiar trepidation. Liz had already seen her and, more importantly, Jessica had seen herself. Yes, she was missing something, but she didn't look like the monster she had made up in her head. In fact, when Liz stood in front of her like that, lust brimming in her eyes, her chest rising and falling rapidly, Jessica didn't think about the prosthesis in one cup of her bra much at all.

Liz took hold of the hem of her own white-and-blue boat-neck top and hoisted it over her head. Jessica was now faced with a real-life bra-clad Liz. Together with that picture above the bed, it made her pulse pick up speed.

Liz brought her hand to Jessica's cheek again and caressed it. Jessica was glad there was no mirror in front of her so she couldn't see how pink her cheeks were.

"You're beautiful," Liz said. Her hand slipped to the back of Jessica's head and she pulled her in for another kiss. It was even more insistent than the last intense one they had shared in the living room. Liz was clearly also very skilled at ratcheting up the tension.

"Do you think I should also hang a naked picture of myself in my bedroom?" Jessica asked when they broke from the kiss, a grin on her face.

"I most certainly do." Liz didn't waste any time and kissed her again. Her hands drifted up Jessica's sides and all the hairs on her skin rose up in excitement. When Liz's hands were on their way down, they halted at the button of Jessica's pants. Liz snapped it open and, in what seemed like one movement, the zipper beneath it as well.

"I want you naked," Liz said, then hesitated for the first time. "As naked as you're comfortable with."

Jessica reached for the button of Liz's jeans and flipped it open. "I'm comfortable with you."

That was what it all came down to in the end. The immense sense of comfort Liz had given her, just by being herself, and being there.

"I'm happy to hear that." Liz pushed Jessica's pants down her hips. She waited for Jessica to do the same to hers.

Jessica wrapped her arms around Liz and drew her nearer to the bed. She took advantage of the situation to unhook Liz's bra.

"Can I take yours off?" Liz whispered in her ears.

Jessica nodded, her chin bumping against Liz's shoulder.

"Okay," Liz said. Before she undid Jessica's bra, she held her close for a while longer. Only after a few more moments of holding her in her strong arms, did she undo Jessica's bra. Jessica held the cups against her while she watched Liz slip her arms out of hers and throw it on a chair behind her.

She swallowed hard at the sight of Liz's naked torso. At the view of her perfect breasts.

Jessica slowly let her bra drop away from her, careful to keep the prosthesis in its cup. She folded it up and gave it to Liz to place down.

Liz laid Jessica's bra on the seat of the chair, treating it with much more care than her own. "Come here," she said.

Jessica stepped into her embrace again and she felt safe and at ease—as at ease as a woman as aroused as her could possibly feel.

Liz kissed her on the cheek and soon Jessica met her lips. As they kissed, Liz walked them to the bed, until Jessica felt the edge bump against the back of her knees.

Liz pushed Jessica onto the bed and crawled on it with her. For Jessica, it felt natural to let Liz take the lead. Liz didn't seem to mind much either. She was probably used to initiating, but no—Jessica willed her thoughts not to go there. This had nothing to do with Liz's profession.

They maneuvered until they were both fully supported by the bed, then Liz pressed her body against Jessica's side.

"Is there anything I'm not allowed to do? Certain spots I'm not allowed to touch?" Liz asked in a soft voice. Her hand rested on Jessica's belly.

Nobody Jessica had ever been in bed with had asked her that question. "I don't mind you touching my breast, but I'm not sure how I'll react to you touching my scar."

"Understood." Liz smiled at her.

Jessica thought it only polite to return the question. "Is there anything I shouldn't—" It sounded so strange, but maybe this was how it should always be. All lines of communication wide open.

"With you, I have zero no-go zones." Liz flashed her a grin, then leaned down to kiss her. She kissed Jessica for a long time, while her hand roamed across her belly and her sides, steering clear of Jessica's chest.

When they finally broke from the kiss, Liz slid half on top of her, pushing her knee between Jessica's legs. She refocused her attention on Jessica's neck, kissing it softly and slowly in a straight line from Jessica's ear to her shoulder. The gentle kisses drove Jessica crazy—and made her forget about how she was lying on her back, totally exposed.

When Liz kissed her like that, and her entire body became one tingling mass, Jessica could almost forget she'd ever had surgery.

Liz moved on to the other side of her neck as Jessica lay squirming underneath her.

Jessica ran her fingers through Liz's straight black hair. It was short in the back and long-ish in the front, so her bangs always threatened to fall into her eyes. She had the most adorable habit of brushing away a strand of hair. And her hair was so soft. As was her skin, although the muscles underneath had nothing of that softness.

Jessica's fingers explored Liz's back. She'd seen it with flexed muscles in that picture above their heads. To now hold that powerful body against hers was a thrill.

Liz kissed a path down from Jessica's neck. Her lips touched down on Jessica's collar bone, then dove south along her left breast. Liz didn't linger but instead started kissing Jessica's belly. It wasn't exactly flabby—Jessica had the good fortune of skinny genes in her family—but it was hardly toned either. Unlike Liz's hard stomach. Maybe she should go to TRX with her.

Liz's tongue dipped into her belly button and the fire that had been steadily building underneath Jessica's skin grew stronger and hotter. Jessica felt she might burst out of her skin soon if Liz kept this up. And she wasn't going to stop any time soon.

It had been a long time since Jessica had really made love to a woman. She'd only met Liz last week, yet she felt like they were making *love*. Liz had helped her take some steps Jessica wasn't sure she could have taken with anyone else—or on her own.

When Liz had shown up on her doorstep instead of Laurel, Jessica's initial disappointment had quickly been replaced by something else entirely. The undeniable chemistry between them.

Jessica felt that chemistry flow through her as Liz kissed her way down from her belly button. She pictured Liz's supple lips touching down on her skin every time their softness sent another pang of arousal up her spine. Soon her thoughts drifted to Liz's tongue, which had felt so heavenly in her mouth, and would feel even more heavenly elsewhere very quickly if Liz kept up this pace.

Jessica shuddered in anticipation. She couldn't believe

how much she wanted this—how much she wanted Liz. And how much Liz wanted her. After she'd just had surgery, feeling sorry for herself in the hospital, she could never have dreamed of anything like this happening to her again. Yet, here she lay. And Liz's lips were closing in.

Liz gently pulled off Jessica's underwear. She pushed Jessica's legs apart and kissed Jessica's inner thigh. Jessica dug her fingers deeper into the flesh of Liz's shoulders. She wished she could feel more of her—she wished she could see her face.

Liz stopped kissing her and looked up. "Are you okay?" she asked.

Jessica gave a quick nod. Liz smiled in response, then resumed her kissing action. She took her time bestowing kiss after kiss on the sensitive skin there and every single one drove up Jessica's level of excitement.

Going to bed with Liz wasn't only exciting because of how she was falling for her, so quickly and unstoppably, but also because of what she did for a living. Jessica could try and deny it as much as she wanted—and she would if asked point blank—but it was extra arousing. Not so much Liz's skill, but all the other implications of her job. The emotional intelligence she had to display. The sensitivity and extreme communication she had to employ. Jessica tried to fight it, but Liz was planting kisses on her thigh—closing in on her wildly pulsing clit—and it was the truth of it. Not a simple truth, but a complex, slightly unnerving one.

Then Liz's tongue touched down on her clit and Jessica stopped thinking altogether. From the moment Liz had given her that first neck massage, this was what Jessica had wanted. This beautiful, smart, strong woman licking her clit. Now it was happening and it met her every expectation.

Jessica buried her fingers in Liz's soft hair. Her entire body felt like a live wire—her clit the spark. She threw her head back and looked at the wall behind her, at the picture of Liz's impressive backside. Then she looked down and saw the part of Liz's back that was curved upward while she was licking her.

It didn't get much better than this. Not after going through a vicious depression, destroying her business, and losing her right breast. For some reason she would never be able to explain, Jessica brought her hand to where her breast used to be. First, she found the void. Then the scar. She planted her hand down on the flattened part of her torso and let it lie there. Her other hand remained in Liz's hair.

For a few moments, Liz stopped licking her clit. Jessica looked down and stared straight into Liz's eyes.

Liz didn't smile, but gave Jessica an altogether different kind of look. One that shivered up Jessica's spine before lodging itself in her heart, in a spot beneath her flesh not far from where her hand was resting on her chest. It was as though Liz had sensed that Jessica had taken the next step and wanted to take time to mark the moment—wanted Jessica to know that she was with her every step of the way.

Liz's head disappeared between Jessica's legs again and her piercing glance was gone. Jessica let her head fall back, kept one hand on her scar, and brought the other one to her left breast, which she cupped gently in her palm. Even though she was in the throes of being sexually pleasured, it wasn't a sexual act. It was one of acceptance.

Liz upped the ante of her licking action. Hot waves of excitement coursed through Jessica's body. This could have happened when they'd first met, but it wouldn't have been the same. It was good that things had played out the way they had. Now, she could meet her orgasm without any reservations. This was right. Liz was right for her. Nothing else mattered.

The back of Jessica's head dug deeper into the pillow.

The burst of heat in the pit of her stomach became unbearable. As she exploded into orgasm, and the blackness behind her eyelids turned into a kaleidoscope of color, an image emerged. Liz looking at her like she had done earlier. Nothing but complete understanding in her glance.

Chapter Seventeen

"Morning," Jessica said. She'd only just opened her eyes and was already met with Liz's gaze on hers.

"Morning, gorgeous." Liz kissed her on the cheek and pressed her naked body against hers.

"Please tell me it's not past eight o'clock yet," Jessica said on a sigh.

"It's just gone seven," Liz said. "Plenty of time to call in sick."

Jessica brought her hands over her eyes. "I really shouldn't. It's irresponsible. It sends the wrong kind of message."

"Come on, Jess. You only live once. And what's the worst that can happen? A Kramer might feel a little less special for a minute or so?"

"God, I hope one day I get the opportunity to introduce you to Kathy Kramer." Jessica crawled deeper into Liz's embrace.

"Tell me, honestly, as a woman who's had cancer and who appreciates the value of every minute of her life... Wouldn't you rather spend the morning with me? If you didn't, you'd miss my super-delicious scrambled eggs, which take time and dedication to prepare."

"Well, I couldn't possibly miss out on your eggs, of course. That would most obviously be a crime against humankind." Jessica removed her hands from over her eyes. "You really are keeping me off the straight and narrow."

"I've never been very interested in the straight and narrow. It's so boring there." Liz's hand stole up Jessica's belly. "And you're too scrumptious to keep to such a boring path."

"I'm sure the HR department at ANBC will agree."

"How about this as a compromise, then." Liz turned on her side and supported her chin on an upturned palm. "Instead of working this morning, you work this afternoon. Sheer brilliance, don't you think?"

"There's just no end to your brilliance." Jessica snickered.

"So, what do you say? Am I allowed to take you hostage in my bed for the morning?"

"Don't you have a TRX class or something?"

"I can do TRX right here." Liz maneuvered under the sheets until she hovered over Jessica. She performed a push-up, lowering herself until her entire front touched Jessica, then pushed herself back up. She repeated the process three times until she collapsed onto Jessica. "Looks like I don't have the strength today, anyway. I'll need to stay in bed to recuperate."

"And the woman is a comedian as well. Where will it end, indeed?" Jessica couldn't suppress a grin from appearing on her lips. She felt so carefree with Liz. But could she really not turn up for work? Without feeling guilty? Because that was bugging her most of all. Maybe she should take a page out of Liz's book. And Liz was right. What was one more morning off work, when you'd had a mastectomy? What if *she* used cancer as an excuse, instead of the cancer using her and turning her into a fearful wallflower?

"I hope it will end with you in this bed for a long time to come," Liz said.

"Okay, fine. I've been officially charmed. You'll need to get your naked body out of bed for a moment and run into the living room to fetch my phone, though," Jessica said.

"Oh really?" Liz, who was still lying half on top of her, slipped off. "Is this how it's going to be?"

"Looks like it. You just told me to enjoy life and to definitely not stay on the straight and narrow. I'm just taking my first steps."

"And I'm not even allowed to wear a robe?" Liz asked.

"Absolutely not." Jessica stuck an arm out from under the duvet. "It's not cold, so that can't be the problem. I hardly think bashfulness is either."

Liz batted her lashes. "For a woman with a naked picture of herself above her bed, I can be extremely bashful."

"Come on." Jessica held up the duvet, letting the warmth escape. "It's up to you."

"Yes, Ma'am." Liz sprang to her feet and gave her behind a little wiggle as she exited the room. She must have sprinted because she was back in a flash, clutching Jessica's purse in front of her chest. "Here you go, Ms. Porter." She handed Jessica the purse and crawled back underneath the covers.

"Thanks." Jessica kissed Liz on the cheek. "Your reward is coming shortly." She fished her phone out of her purse and looked at the screen. "It's not even seven thirty yet. It's too early to call."

"You tricked me." Liz started tickling her. "You have to pay."

Liz's hands were so cold that Jessica dropped the phone.

"Stop it," she squealed. "I'll email my assistant. She'll take care of it."

Liz stopped tickling her. "Go on. You have two minutes before my hands are all over you again."

Jessica shook her head. She composed a quick email and sent it before she could change her mind.

"How does it feel?" Liz asked.

Jessica put the phone away and turned to Liz. "You make it sound as though skiving off work is the most daring thing I've ever done."

Liz waggled her eyebrows. "Do tell. What is the most daring thing you've ever done?"

Jessica should have known Liz would call her bluff. She was that kind of person. Jessica racked her brain. She wasn't sure she could share the most daring experience she'd had. But this was Liz. She felt she could tell her just about anything—after having revealed her scar—and making love to her.

"I'll have you know I had a foursome once." She tried to look smug, but guessed she probably just looked ridiculous, what with words like that coming from her mouth—they didn't quite fit.

"What? Hold the presses!" Liz sat up. "Give me all the details, please."

Jessica chuckled. "I can't give you all the details. That would be breaking the confidence of those involved."

"Really? Were they women of whom one would not suspect they would be involved in such an activity? Like one Jessica Porter?"

Jessica thought about that. "No, actually not at all. It was definitely the most daring and unexpected experience for me, even though I was the one who set it up."

Liz looked at her expectantly and Jessica told her the story of how, not long after she received her cancer diagnosis, she organized a dinner party at her home with Katherine, Caitlin, and Jo. And how one thing had led to another.

"Caitlin James?" Liz asked, after Jessica had finished her story. "You slept with Caitlin James?"

"You sound impressed." Jessica couldn't suppress a smile.

"Let's just say there aren't many Australians who are so vocal and eloquent about some very important topics. I don't admire many people, but I definitely admire her."

Jessica glanced at Liz, but didn't say anything.

Liz cocked her head in response.

"I talked to Caitlin about you and… if you play your cards right, you might very well be invited to dinner at hers and Jo's on Saturday."

"Hm," Liz said. "Please remind me, which card game is it again that we're playing?" She sneaked her finger up Jessica's thigh gently, then started tickling her again.

"Stop, stop. It's too early for this," Jessica groaned.

"Does that mean the invitation is now official?" Liz stared at her with hope in her eyes.

"I'd love for you to join us. Although I'll need to tell Katherine first." Jessica's shoulders slumped.

"Katherine?" Liz knitted her brows together. "Wait, that dinner party you just told me about… and this upcoming one. Are they of the *same kind*?" She put emphasis on the last two words.

"What? No. We're all friends now. That was a one-time thing. A goodbye-to-my-right-breast tumble in the hay. Caitlin and I have gotten way too close to repeat that. She really stood by me after I had my surgery. Everything's different now between us." Jessica put a hand on Liz's wrist. "Besides, I don't want to share you."

"In that case I'd be very happy to join you," Liz said.

"You're free?" Jessica asked, unsure whether she was successfully hiding the trepidation in her voice.

"Even if I wasn't, I'd make sure I was." Liz smiled at her. "So what's the deal with Katherine?"

"She gave me a speech about how utterly stupid it would be for me to develop feelings for you."

"You told Katherine about me as well?" Liz waggled her eyebrows. They were long and very expressive. "My name has been rolling off some tongues, it seems." She chuckled.

"I just told her that you replaced Laurel. I didn't tell her anything. She just assumed."

"Did she now?" Liz scooted a little closer to Jessica. "She has the sixth sense. It probably makes her very good at what she does."

"She wasn't very understanding about it."

"That makes perfect sense to me." Liz shot her an apologetic smile. "She wouldn't be a very good friend if she encouraged you to have the hots for the likes of me."

It was Jessica's turn to arch up her eyebrows.

"Let's face it. The reason Laurel left is either that she was ready for retirement or she met someone who couldn't deal with what she was doing for a living. That's the reality of this job," Liz said. "Katherine knows these things. She wants to save you from getting hurt. It's normal. She's just trying to be a good friend to you. Something you can hardly hold against her."

"Yet here I am. In bed with you." Jessica couldn't quite believe what she was hearing. "And I don't need saving."

"Hey." Liz swung an arm across Jessica's belly and held her close. "This is going to come up. Your friends will have questions. Although, perhaps, we're getting just a tad ahead of ourselves."

Jessica relaxed her shoulders and let herself fall into the mattress a little deeper. She hadn't gotten that much sleep and she was still tired—her body stiff in places she didn't even know it could be.

"Didn't you promise me your super-delicious scrambled eggs?" she said.

"I sure did." Liz kissed her on the tip of the nose. "Do we need to talk about this more?"

Jessica shook her head. "Not now. It's not even eight and someone kept me up most of the night."

"Really? I wonder who that was?" Liz grinned at her again—that irresistible disarming grin. She wondered how many women got wet just at the sight of it?

"The same woman who promised me eggs for breakfast."

"Ah, you mean the same woman who made you dinner?"

"And gave me a few orgasms in between." Jessica felt herself relax again.

"Christ, what a woman."

Jessica nodded. "The kind that truly deserves a picture of herself above her own bed." She chuckled.

"I know all about that kind." Liz nuzzled her neck and, instantly, Jessica was flooded with memories of last night again.

Chapter Eighteen

"ALL YOU NEED IS patience and a generous dollop of butter," Liz said. She cracked a couple of eggs into a bowl and started whisking. She wore a tight tank top and Jessica was entranced by the slight flex in her biceps as she spun the fork around.

Liz was the kind of woman Jessica could look at for days on end. Study the ripple of her muscles, the smoothness of her skin. She looked at least ten years younger than her age.

"What's your secret?" Jessica motioned with her hand to cover the entire length of Liz's body. "How come you look like this at thirty-nine?"

Liz looked up from her eggs. "I treat my body the way certain gay men treat theirs." She winked. "I save my calories for alcohol."

Jessica chuckled.

"I'm serious," Liz said. "And this being Bondi, my TRX class is usually a bunch of gay guys and me."

"Sounds like fun."

"It's a hoot afterward." She poured the eggs into the pan.

"Now, no more distractions, please. It's all in the attention you give the scramble."

"These eggs are so hyped. I hope you're not setting me up for disappointment," Jessica joked.

"I've never had one negative review of my eggs, so best brace yourself."

Jessica watched Liz as she stirred the eggs. "Are you doing anything special to them? It doesn't look any different than ordinary scrambled eggs."

"Shh," Liz said. "I need to focus and you're very distracting."

Jessica watched her in silence. Below the black tank top, Liz was wearing a stripy pair of pajama bottoms. She looked so scrumptious, Jessica would rather have another piece of her than those eggs she was scrambling.

She got up from her chair and stood behind Liz, wrapping her arms around her, and letting her hands slip underneath Liz's tank top.

"What did I tell you?" Liz said, but her voice sounded mellow and she leaned into Jessica's embrace. "Besides, if you're going to spend the morning here, you need to eat because you'll need your strength." Liz pushed her behind against Jessica's groin. She wasn't wearing any underwear beneath her pajama bottoms and Jessica let one hand slide inside her pants to cup her ass cheek.

"Okay, that's the eggs ruined." Liz switched off the gas and put the pan on another hob. She turned around, removing Jessica's arm from her trousers. "When I'm cooking, I become highly combustible, so you'd better fuck me now." There was no smile on her face, only determination. Lust glimmered in her eyes. She reached for Jessica's forearm and slid Jessica's hand back into her pants. "Please finish what you started." The words seemed to come from deep inside her throat.

"But I'm hungry," Jessica said. Her hand swept past Liz's pubic hair, straight for the prize.

"You should have thought of that before you got handsy with me." Liz grinned at her. "Anyway, I've got just the thing to still your most acute hunger." She pushed her pants down.

At the sight of her own hand between Liz's legs, Jessica's pulse picked up speed.

"Fuck me," Liz said, and she said it in such a way that Jessica couldn't do anything else—not that she had any other plans.

Jessica kissed Liz on the lips. Those soft, soft lips that could draw into the most gorgeous smile. What had she called it? A TV smile. The country would be a better place if Liz's smile was broadcast to its people on a regular basis, of this Jessica was convinced.

With her finger, she stroked along Liz's nether lips. She remembered the sight of them from last night. Everything about Liz was just so excruciatingly beautiful. No exceptions.

Liz stepped out of her pajama bottoms, then she spread her legs wider. Jessica took advantage of the better access to slip the tip of her finger a little higher up Liz's lips, to gauge for wetness. She was surprised to be met with a copious amount.

"How is this even possible?" she whispered in Liz's ear when they broke from their kiss.

"Must have been whisking the eggs." Liz shot her a quick grin, then pulled her back in for a kiss.

Jessica slipped her finger higher inside of Liz. Automatically, memories of last night blasted her mind. Her hand on her scar as Liz made her come. The ultimate act of accepting that this was who she was now. A woman with one remaining breast. It felt as though Liz had given her that gift of acceptance. For that reason, as Jessica slipped another one of her fingers inside Liz, she was able to easily shove aside any worries about not being the only one to do this to Liz in the weeks, perhaps even months or years, to come.

Liz clutched Jessica's shoulder with one hand. They broke from the kiss and Jessica scanned her face. A small smile played on her lips. Jessica moved slowly inside of her. Liz seemed to be enjoying the rhythm.

"I want you to make me come like this," Liz whispered. "Just by fucking me with your fingers."

Jessica smiled at her. That was a new one. Liz was still so new to her. Jessica wasn't all that acquainted with her body yet. And she was fucking her against the stove, of which at least one hob was still hot from Liz's attempt at making eggs.

But if Jessica had learned one thing in her forty-five years on this planet, it was to fake it until she made it. She narrowed her eyes and tried to empty her mind. Overthinking it wasn't going to help—that would only make her feel like she was taking some sort of exam. *Make the call girl come.* Wait. Was that why Liz was talking to her like that? No. *Stop it.* Jessica had two fingers inside the most gorgeous woman she had—truly—ever seen. A woman who had just begged her to make her come. A woman who already meant so much to her.

Liz started meeting her thrusts while grinding herself onto Jessica's fingers, giving Jessica the impression that she'd be taking care of her own climax. Jessica's fingers were just the instrument she needed to get there. Jessica hoped something more than an instrument was needed. Perhaps the connection between them. And the look in Jessica's eyes as she fucked Liz.

Liz kept her eyes open throughout. Her teeth sank into her bottom lip as Jessica's fingers and Liz's pussy seemed to melt from two separate body parts, from two different human beings, into one entity. They moved together. Jessica could feel Liz's growing arousal shoot up through her fingers. She felt it tingle inside of her. She lost herself in the lust she saw in Liz's eyes. Because that was what had gotten her this far along the way. The fact that Liz wanted her. It was in her every word, in her every glance. It was reflected back perfectly at Jessica now as she looked into Liz's eyes. Those pools of kindness mixed with kinkiness. Jessica couldn't get enough of them. Certainly not now when her fingers were being swallowed by the heat of Liz's pussy.

"Oh, Jess," Liz moaned. Her fingers dug deeper into Jessica's shoulder muscles. So deeply, Jessica guessed they would leave a mark, but she didn't mind a mark left by Liz. Liz stopped grinding and her eyes fell shut while she shivered and let out a few deep-throated sighs.

She breathed out heavily through her nose as her limbs relaxed and Jessica withdrew her fingers.

"You can forget about those eggs now," Liz said. "Unless you enjoy eating rubber." She pulled Jessica into a hug and kissed her on the mouth.

Chapter Nineteen

JESSICA PACED around her living room. She stopped at the window and looked out across the street. No sign of Katherine yet. She'd invited her over for two reasons. To tell her about Liz. And to get the scolding she knew she was going to get. She needed it. It was Friday evening and Liz was *working* and the thought of it was doing Jessica's head in. She didn't know what to do with herself. She didn't know what to think. She tried to keep certain images from popping up in her head, but it didn't work. She'd wandered around her living room unstoppably since 7 p.m.—the time Liz had *gone to work*.

Jessica was still standing by the window when a car pulled up. It was Katherine's white Audi. Jessica took a deep breath and headed for the front door.

She opened it before Katherine had a chance to ring the bell.

Before she hugged Jessica, she said, "Are you okay, Jess? You haven't had any bad news, have you?" Katherine pulled her into a tight hug.

"I'm fine. Come in." She ushered Katherine into the

living room. They sat down but Jessica immediately stood up again. "Drink?" she asked.

Katherine narrowed her eyes and regarded her. "Something's going on. What is it?"

"I'll tell you over a drink, shall I?" Jessica said.

"Sure. I'll have some of that wine you're drinking."

Jessica had opened a bottle right after she'd called Katherine and asked her to meet. She'd gone through nearly half of it on her own.

She tried to take a discreet deep breath as she poured Katherine some wine.

"Okay," she said. "You're going to think I've lost my mind and I actually very much think I am losing my mind." She fidgeted with the sleeve of her sweater. "Just for the record."

Katherine slanted her head. "Let me guess," she said. "You've only gone and fallen in love with an escort."

Jessica sighed. "We just really clicked."

"Oh, I'm sure you did." Katherine drank from the wine Jessica had just poured her. "I'm not going to judge you for falling for her, but don't expect this to be a walk in the park either."

Jessica sighed. "I know it's not. I'm going mad because, er, right at this moment Liz is with a client. Honestly, if you weren't here, I'm not sure what I would be doing."

Katherine put down her glass. "Look, Jess, I wish there was a manual for this, but there isn't. If you're going to do this with Liz—have a relationship with her—you're going to have to tell her how you feel, but you're also going to have to learn to respect what she does and that she chose this job." She looked longingly at her glass again. "Believe me, I know it's hard."

"If I'm going to be like this three times a week…" Jessica said.

"You're freaking out right now. It's normal. You probably have all sorts of images in your head."

"Not only that, but I have a pit the size of a cannonball in my stomach. If I see her tomorrow, what am I going to say to her? How am I going to behave? I mean… I'm jealous. That's really what it comes down to."

"Oh, Jess. Of all the women in Sydney." Katherine shot her a smile.

"She just… made me feel something so real, so undeniable. We had fun, you know. Genuine fun. She made me giggle when I didn't think I had much reason to." She pulled up her shoulders. "I just love being around her. I love how she makes me feel when I'm with her. And she seems to feel the same way."

"All of that, eh?" Katherine said warily.

"And then some. I just wonder what she sees in me."

Katherine held up her hand. "Oh no, none of that, please. It's well established you're a catch."

"The hell I am."

"I'm not even going to discuss that. Honestly, you can take that up with Mrs. Buchman. I've wasted enough of my breath on trying to convince you of that."

Jessica waved off Katherine's remark. "I invited Liz to Caitlin's." While she had her hand up, she gestured for Katherine to swallow her upcoming remark. "Don't worry, it was Caitlin who extended the invitation. She knows what Liz does. I told her."

"I look forward to getting to know her better then." Katherine cocked her head. "And to seeing the two of you together."

"Have you and her ever, er, worked together?"

Katherine chuckled. "Please, Jess, don't ask *me* these questions. Ask them of Liz. Start a conversation. Whatever it is you and she are starting, it's not going to be easy, but it sure as hell won't be boring either. You'll always have plenty to talk about."

"Thank goodness we'll have conversation then."

"Conversation is a lot to have."

They sat pondering this for a moment.

"I thought you'd be more cross with me," Jessica said. "That you'd go off the deep end like last time."

"That was hardly me going off the deep end. Either way, it needed to be said. This isn't a fairytale you're walking into."

"Maybe not, but she's as gorgeous as any fairy princess." A smile appeared on her lips. "I guess when you look like that, you might as well…" Jessica brought a hand to her mouth. Had she really said that out loud?

Katherine either hadn't heard or had decided to ignore Jessica's last remark. She didn't say anything and Jessica couldn't bear the silence hanging between them.

"Do you think it's possible… I mean, do you know women who do what you do and are in a successful relationship?" Jessica asked.

Katherine reached for her wine glass again. She drank before speaking. "Don't you think it's time you actually started using the words invented for *what it is I do*? I'm an escort, Jess. Some would call me a hooker, or a call girl, a prostitute or a sex worker."

"There's no need to be crass," Jessica blurted out.

"It's not crass. It's a job."

Jessica let her head fall back. "I'm sorry," she said when she looked back up. "I didn't mean to offend you. It was just all so much easier before I met Liz."

"To answer your question. Yes, it is possible, but not common. But there are always exceptions to the rule."

"Liz wants to start an art gallery," Jessica said. "I have

money." She regretted it as soon as the words had left her mouth.

"Please don't try to save her. Liz doesn't need saving. Please take the advice I'm about to give you very seriously. Don't offer her money. One of the core reasons any of us do this job is because of the independence it gives us. We don't need some rich girl swooping in with bags of money. We make our own way." She took a quick sip. "I can only speak for myself, of course."

"You don't have to tell me you can't buy happiness with money," Jessica said. "My father's been trying that all his life and he isn't exactly the happiest person I know."

"Would this include you as well?" Katherine asked.

"Well, I certainly know," Jessica said wistfully. "I've experienced it firsthand. But money is supposed to make some things easier." Of course, the simple equation of her having money and Liz saving money to open her own art gallery didn't work in real life. Jessica knew that much as well.

"You're going to need to have a cold hard look in the mirror and ask yourself if being with Liz is what you really want. It's going to come at a price. Are you willing to pay?"

"There's no way I'm letting her go because she's an… escort." She barely managed to squeeze the last word past her lips. "She makes me feel too good—too much—for that."

"Think about it for a bit longer, anyway. Because this is the early stage, when you're still giddy with hormones which make a lot of things a lot easier to handle."

"I showed her my scar, Kat. Somehow, she got me to do that. Before I hadn't even dared to look at myself in the mirror."

"You did?" Katherine's eyes grew wide.

Jessica nodded. "It was such a special moment, but when you look at it in another way… I mean, I *had* booked her. It could also be something totally different. Like a paid-for emotion or something."

"There's no such thing as a paid-for emotion," Katherine said matter-of-factly.

"You know what I mean." Jessica looked at her friend. She probably had a lesson or two to learn from her. Maybe Katherine was right and she should be learning them from the woman she was falling in love with instead.

"I know what you're getting at, but I think it's a pretty safe bet that what you felt when you showed yourself to Liz was as real as it gets. There's no way that didn't evoke some very real emotions in her. It might very well be why she's falling in love with you. Vulnerability can be a beautiful thing."

Out of nowhere, a tear pushed itself out of the corner of Jessica's eye. "Oh, fuck." She quickly wiped it away. "I haven't cried since…" She had to think. "Since before the surgery."

"Oh, Jess." Katherine stood and came to sit next to her in the couch. "Why are you rich people so hard on yourselves?"

"I don't think it's necessarily a privilege of the privileged," she joked. She didn't want any more tears leaking from her eyes.

"From what I gather, what happened between you and Liz was a beautiful thing. You opened yourself up to her emotionally and that's not an easy thing to do. No matter how difficult things might be, you'll always have that." Katherine put her arms around Jessica. "I think you should have a good cry on my shoulder now. I'm your friend, remember?" She rubbed a finger over the fabric of her blouse. "This old thing can take it."

Jessica shook her head. "I don't want to cry."

"If you're sure." Katherine pulled her a little closer. "Either way, I'm here."

Jessica put her head on Katherine's shoulder. She swallowed the rest of her tears and thanked her lucky stars Katherine had come over. But, of course, she couldn't call a friend every time Liz went to see a client. If this was going to last, she'd need to find a different coping mechanism.

Chapter Twenty

"HEY GORGEOUS." Liz kissed Jessica on the cheek. It was a lingering kiss and Jessica inhaled Liz's scent deeply.

They had a few hours before they were expected at Caitlin and Jo's. Jessica was glad they had some time together. After last night's agitation, she felt she needed to get used to being around Liz again. It seemed to be a recurring thing. She always managed to feel completely at ease with Liz, but only after a while. Before she could reach that stage, she always had to take on a certain hurdle—it wasn't much of a secret to Jessica what the problem was.

They headed into the sitting room and sat down. Liz had proposed to meet at the Pink Bean, but Jessica had asked her to come over to her house instead. She needed to say a few things and wasn't sure a Saturday afternoon at the Pink Bean was the best location for it—not that there was any best location to have this particular conversation.

"I missed you." Liz apparently didn't have any hurdles to overcome because she started pushing Jessica down into the couch. "A lot." She went straight for her neck.

"Please, stop," Jessica said, in a more forceful tone than she wanted to.

Liz sat up and looked at her. "What's going on? I figured you didn't want to meet me in the coffee shop because…" She waggled her eyebrows. "You know."

Jessica scoffed.

"What?" Liz asked.

"You really don't know?" Jessica asked.

Liz sighed. She adjusted her position and sat down properly, crossing one knee over the other.

"I have an informed guess." She fixed her gaze on Jessica. "Talk to me."

Jessica huffed out some air. "Talk, talk, talk," she said. "Some things just aren't that easy to talk about. Some things, I simply don't have the vocabulary for."

"Well, I *do*, Jess." Liz turned in the couch, drawing one leg up. "You're jealous. It's to be expected."

"I—I just have no idea how to deal with this—how to be around you."

"Ask me what you want to know. I'll tell you. I can't tell you who I was with, but I can tell you what happened. Is that what you want to know?"

Jessica considered this, but the ball in the pit of her stomach only seemed to grow at the thought of actually knowing what Liz and her client had been up to. She shook her head. "No, I guess that, for starters, I just want to know if with… your client, it was the same as with me."

"Of course it wasn't. How could it possibly be?"

"I was your client," Jessica said.

"For about five minutes, Jess. I think we both knew there was something else going on between us pretty quickly." Liz looked away for a moment, then fixed her gaze on Jessica again. "People meet under all sorts of circumstances and this happens to be how we met. I've never fallen for a client before and I didn't fall for you because you were a client. But what you have to understand is that I no longer justify what I do, because doing that would mean a few things. For starters, it would mean that it *needs* justifying. In the end, I could give you all the justification I wanted, it wouldn't change how you felt. I can understand how you feel, that's not what I'm saying, but this is something you're going to have to get over. I'll help you in any way I can, but this is me. This is what I do and what I'm going to be doing for the foreseeable future. Either you learn to live with it or you don't."

"I'm sorry," Jessica said. "I didn't think it was going to be this hard."

"It's okay. You'll get used to it."

Jessica wasn't so sure of that. How could she possibly get used to the woman she was falling in love with sleeping with other people? But then again, what choice did she have? Stop falling in love? If this couldn't stop her, nothing would.

"Maybe we need some sort of protocol," Jessica said, even though she didn't really know where she was going with this suggestion. "Some cooling off period after you've had a date with a client."

Liz shook her head. "How about this instead." She shuffled closer but didn't touch Jessica. "I just don't tell you when I'm working. That way you can't freak out about it."

"I'm not sure that's going to work. I'll know regardless of you telling me."

"Oh really? Have you been bestowed with the gift of knowing what I'm up to when we're not together?"

"If you're not free in the evening, I won't be able to conclude otherwise than that you're on a date."

"That's your conclusion to draw, but I do have other evening activities. Gym. Friends. Art show openings. Believe it or not, I have a life. A good one. One I'd introduce you to, if I felt you were up to it."

"That's a bit unfair." Jessica shuffled in her seat. "You can't blame me for how I feel."

"I don't blame you. I just wish we could move past this." Liz held out her hand.

Jessica looked at it. Suddenly, holding each other's hand had taken on a deeper meaning. If she put her hand in Liz's, it meant she was at least willing to give that a try. That she was willing to consider moving past it.

She extended her hand and touched Liz's. Immediately, the softness of it struck her again, but the knot in her stomach remained.

"Shall I impart some hooker wisdom on you?" Liz shot her a soft smile.

"Please do," Jessica said. That smile was making her melt already.

"It's all a balancing act. Basically, life is a balancing act. We're all just looking for the same thing. It's not so much about happiness as about a steadier feeling of contentment. That's the balance. But every time the pendulum swings one way, be it to the side of extreme happiness or extreme sadness, or any other off-balance emotion, it needs to swing all the way back to the other side if it ever wants to reach the middle again." With the finger of her free hand, Liz made a swinging motion, then halted in a spot in the air that was supposed to be the middle. "One doesn't exist without the other. You want to be with me." Her finger went up in the air. "But for that to happen you'll have to accept certain parts of me, which will be a challenge." Her finger arched to the other side of where it had previously stopped. "But hopefully we'll meet each other here at some point." Her finger curved through the air and stopped at Liz's self-chosen point of balance.

"Wow." Jessica chuckled because she didn't really know how else to react. "Very deep for a hooker, indeed."

"See, you're starting to swing the other way already. You just made a hooker joke." Liz's smile grew—it resembled the arc she had drawn in the air.

Chapter Twenty-One

"I HAVE BROUGHT A FAN GIRL," Jessica said before she introduced Liz to Caitlin. "Brace yourself."

"I can keep my cool," Liz said, and held out her hand to Caitlin. "Unlike some."

Jessica saw her wink at Caitlin. Caitlin responded with a big smile followed by ignoring Liz's extended hand and drawing her into a hug instead.

"This is my partner Jo," she said, and put a hand on Jo's shoulder.

"I've heard a lot about you," Liz said and, following Caitlin's lead, threw her arms around Jo.

"Very nice to meet you," Jo said.

As Jessica kissed Jo hello, she wondered if Caitlin had told her about what Liz did for a living. Then she remembered what Katherine had told her the other day. She should stop referring to Liz's profession in roundabout ways—even in her own head—if she was ever going to accept it, which, truth be told, Jessica wasn't so sure she could.

"Katherine texted she's going to be late," Caitlin said. "It's just us for now. Do come through."

Jessica had been at Caitlin and Jo's before, but she let Liz take in the place in her own time. And it was a hell of a place to take in. Jessica remembered the very first time she'd been invited here. She'd like to believe that she'd set up that foursome all by herself, but Caitlin had propositioned her first. In this very place.

The memory of that evening, strangely, put Jessica more at ease. Perhaps because it reminded her of Caitlin's extreme lack of judgement when it came to certain things. If she could take Liz as her date somewhere for the first time, it was here. Jessica didn't want to think ahead to the moment when she would introduce Liz to her father. His first question to anyone was, without exception, "What do you do for a living?"

They all sat in the living room. Liz cast a glance at Caitlin and Jo's impressive bookshelf. Jo poured champagne without asking if everyone wanted to have the same drink.

Jessica took a sip immediately, just to calm her nerves. Wasn't this going a little too fast? It was the worst time to wonder about this, because the invitation had been accepted and they were already sitting on Caitlin and Jo's couch, but she wondered nonetheless. Should she be introducing Liz to her friends already? It had seemed logical after their first week together, but that was before Liz had been with a client. Those few hours had changed a lot for Jessica.

She tried to hold on to the sweet memories she and Liz had already created, and how important those memories already were in her life. But was it really worth all this insecurity?

Earlier at home, Liz had wanted to make love, but Jessica couldn't even consider it. Even though Liz looked as scrumptious as ever, and her smile was confident and inviting, her body just as strong-looking as always. There was a mental barrier Jessica wasn't able to overcome.

She needed to find a way to relax. Or perhaps Caitlin and Jo would help. After all, Jessica had been as relaxed as she could possibly be around them. Yet the thought of that didn't seem to help. Instead, it blended together in her brain as one big mess of strange memories and too high expectations and a question that made its way forward through all the fog in her mind: since when had sex become so important? Since when was it allowed to influence her thoughts and conversations so much? Christ, Jessica should get a grip.

"Are you okay, Jess?" Jo asked.

All three of them were holding up their glass. Jessica had missed the toast.

"Yes." She tried to sound assured. "Cheers. Thanks for having us."

―――――

Katherine arrived and Caitlin had served dinner not long after. The fact that she was in charge of the main course didn't seem to stop Caitlin from knocking back quite a few glasses of champagne, making Jessica wonder whether she was nervous about something.

Liz, Katherine, Jo and Caitlin seemed to be having a great time, with conversation flowing easily and sometimes, apparently, hilariously, between them. Jessica didn't seem to get half of the jokes and innuendo. Not tonight.

"I'm not sure what my life would be like without my gays," Liz said. "No offense to anyone present, of course, but lesbians can be so bloody uptight."

"None taken," Caitlin was the first to say. "I'm pretty sure you don't mean me."

"Nor me," Katherine chimed in. "I can't really afford to be."

Jo clutched a hand to her chest. "What? I'm the

uptight one then?" She shook her head. "I guess I used to be, but I'd like to believe I've unwound quite a bit since shacking up with Caitlin. Who wouldn't? What with the things she makes me do." She grinned and blew Caitlin a kiss.

Caitlin shot Jo a wink.

"You're awfully quiet tonight, Jess," Caitlin said. "Are you all right?" She leaned over the table. "You're sworn to complete openness when it comes to your health, with both Kat and me. You scared us too much when you disappeared on us three months ago." She looked at Liz. "Has she told you about that?"

"She has." Liz put a hand in the small of Jessica's back. Jessica hated herself for flinching. She hoped Liz hadn't noticed, but Liz noticed everything. To make up for it, she pushed her back into the palm of Liz's hand, only to feel her retract it abruptly.

"I'm fine. I promise you. I had an appointment with my oncologist last Thursday. Everything's going according to plan. I just had a bit of a weird week with going back to work."

"Understandable," Jo said. She was such a sweetheart. And she was about to get her PhD. Now *that* was respectable. You could take that information home and boast about it to your parents.

"I hope you don't think I meant that you're uptight, Jess." Liz was sitting next to her and turned toward her. She gave Jessica a look she couldn't quite decipher.

"Of course not," Jessica quickly said.

"It's not every day you have dinner with two call girls," Caitlin said, which was such a typical thing for her to say.

Jessica froze. She took a deep breath and tried to relax. Everyone else at the table seemed to find this amusing. It was easy enough for Caitlin to say. Her girlfriend was the very picture of wholesomeness. Although even Jo was chuckling away happily.

Jessica realized she had been talking to the wrong people about this. Katherine and Caitlin were much more open-minded than she was. She needed someone to confide in about this who would have an equally hard time dealing with it. But, of course, that would make the conversation so much harder to have. What would be the benefit in the end? Jessica's unease would just be strengthened.

By the time Jessica snapped out of the tailspin of her thoughts, the conversation had progressed. She looked to her left, where Liz was sitting. Was it her imagination or had Liz moved her chair away from her? Either way, whether there was more physical distance between them or not, Jessica felt a huge emotional divide opening up.

"It's just another double standard in today's society," Josephine was saying. "I'm guilty of it as well. It takes work to get past that sort of thing." She cleared her throat. "I was all up in arms when I found out that Katherine was a sex worker, *after* I slept with her, I must add." She shot Caitlin a look.

"Understandably so," Caitlin said. "I should have told you." She glanced at Jessica.

"I should have said something," Jessica said. "It wasn't fair."

"Well, yes. Information is always paramount," Jo said. "But my point is that I got over it very quickly. Once I knew what Katherine's situation was, it didn't matter to me that much."

"Wait," Liz said. "There's something I'm missing here." She glanced at Jessica. "You told me that the four of you got it on and that you set it up as some sort of pre-mastectomy 'treat'."

Jessica nodded. It sounded so silly when put like that.

"So why did Kat's job matter? Wasn't it just four friends getting together?" She narrowed her eyes. "Or did you book Katherine to spice up your evening? And didn't tell Caitlin and Jo?"

"That's right. Jess sprang that one on us well and good," Caitlin said. "I worked it out pretty quickly, but Jo didn't."

Liz raised her eyebrows and leaned back in her chair. Jessica felt the distance between them loom even larger than before.

Jessica wanted nothing more than to change the topic of conversation. She glanced at Josephine. "Jo, how's your thesis coming along?"

"Oh no, we don't mention the T-word on a Saturday evening," Caitlin said. "It's crunch time for Jo." She drew Jo close to her by the shoulder. "But she needs to relax tonight." She kissed Jo on the cheek making a big smacking sound.

"It's a bit stressful at the moment," Jo said. She leaned into Caitlin's embrace. Their closeness made the gap between Jessica and Liz appear even greater.

"Is work totally not allowed as a topic?" Liz asked. She looked at Jessica pointedly while doing so—as though she was setting all the rules.

"No, of course not." Jessica tried a smile. She fought the urge to scoot her chair a little closer to Liz's—to bridge that growing distance between them. She wished they hadn't come here. That they'd just stayed home and enjoyed each other's company. "We can talk about anything."

"Good, because I'm about to have a fan girl moment." Liz turned to Caitlin. "You once wrote something about sex workers. I read it just after I had made the decision to join The Lesbian Experience and it made me feel so much better about myself and my decision." Liz tapped a finger against her chin. "I'm trying to remember the exact words. I can usually recite them by heart, but I think I've had a bit too much of this." She pointed at her empty glass.

"Sex work isn't always a manifestation of exploitation, abuse, or a dysfunctional power dynamic. It can be empowering and a viable way to make a living," Katherine said.

"Yes, that's it." Liz smiled at Katherine, who sat opposite her. "That was some sturdy hooker pep talk. But not just that. You made me feel as though we mattered just as much as anyone else. That what we do is equally important and viable as any other services provided for money. It was very significant to read for me at the time."

"There are so many different kinds of sex work," Caitlin said. "What you and Katherine do is light years away from what ninety-nine percent of the population think it is. And of course sex work can also be exploitative. It can put the people who do it in a very vulnerable position. They face violence and degrading circumstances every single day. It has never been my objective to sugarcoat things and to make it look like it's all sunshine and roses, because it's not. But when it's your own choice and you have a very clear reason for doing it—and that reason is mostly money—then it shouldn't be automatically judged."

"If you don't mind me asking," Jo said. "Have either of you ever worked with men?"

Both Liz and Katherine shook their heads vigorously.

"We provide The Lesbian Experience only," Katherine said.

"I'm sure there are plenty of men who'd like to put themselves right in the middle of that," Caitlin said.

Liz rolled her eyes. "Been there, *not* done that."

Jessica glanced at Liz. There was so much she didn't know—so much she would never know.

"Alana has a knack for sniffing out weird situations," Katherine said.

"Alana is the owner of the agency," Liz explained. "Sometimes she does make mistakes, though." Liz grinned at Jessica. "But hey, if she weren't human and prone to mistakes just like the rest of us, I would never have met Jess." She shot Jessica the most endearing smile. "Nor would I be sitting at Caitlin James and Josephine Greenwood's dinner table."

"Alana really screwed that one up," Katherine said. "That should never have happened."

Liz shrugged. "Maybe it happened for a reason."

Jessica tried to smile, but her lips remained in a pout. A cock-up at an escort agency. That was her and Liz's origin story. She could just imagine the faces of her family members when she told them.

"Maybe," Jessica said. Then the ugliest thought she'd had so far crossed her mind. Why, after all the hardship she had gone through during the past year, when she'd finally met someone she really liked, did the object of her affection have to be a hooker?

Chapter Twenty-Two

"CAN I COME IN?" Liz asked, when they reached Jessica's house. They had walked back in silence from Caitlin's apartment in Darlinghurst. It was only a fifteen-minute walk. All throughout, Jessica had tried to focus on the memory of the first walks she and Liz had taken. The unexpectedly pleasant meanderings though her neighborhood. But her mind had been persistent and had not allowed her to dwell on those innocent dates they'd had.

"Of course." Jessica opened the door and let them in. Liz was in no state to drive home and Jessica guessed it was implied that she would stay the night.

"I don't just want to assume," Liz said. She seemed to have a particular liking for champagne and had happily guzzled up anything Caitlin had much too generously poured. Since her surgery, Jessica seemed to have gone off champagne and she'd only drank a few sips to be polite.

When Jessica closed the door behind them, Liz immediately pushed Jessica's back against it. "I've been waiting to do this all night," she said. She wasn't so drunk that she slurred her words. She just looked pleasantly tipsy, really, yet her very demeanor was getting on Jessica's nerves.

Liz nibbled on her neck, then traced a path of wet kisses to Jessica's cheek, to land on her lips.

Jessica didn't open her mouth to let Liz's tongue slip in.

Liz withdrew and looked at her. "Not in the mood?" she asked.

"Not really."

"What's wrong?" Liz scrutinized her face and Jessica could barely stand Liz's gaze on her.

"Nothing. I'm just tired."

"Would you rather I went home?" Liz took a step back. "I can call a taxi."

Jessica sighed. "I don't know."

"If you don't know then I should probably go."

Jessica didn't say anything because she was afraid confirming would lead to something she might regret, but she couldn't deny that she wanted Liz to go home. She tried to remember Liz's words about the swinging pendulum, but her brain was too tired and foggy.

Liz brought her hands to her hips. "You're not going to say anything?"

"I don't know what to say. Okay? I have no idea."

"How about you say what's going through your mind right this second." Liz's voice was no longer smooth, nor calm.

"I—I just don't want to—" Jessica stopped. "Why don't you come in and we'll talk about it." She moved farther into the hallway past Liz.

"Talk some more? I'm not in the mood for that, Jess. It's late. We can talk tomorrow." Liz's shoulders sagged.

"I just can't be with you right now. I need some time to… I don't know, to process, I guess."

"If you're so afraid to say it, then why don't I pick up

your slack, huh?" Liz squared her shoulders. "Don't think I didn't notice you were ashamed of me."

"I wasn't ashamed of you." The high pitch in Jessica's voice betrayed her lie.

"Come on, Jess. Be honest. It's the only way," Liz pleaded.

"I'm sorry." She sighed. "All I seem to be doing is apologizing for how I feel. It's making me so ill at ease. I don't want to feel this way. I don't want our first weeks together to be like this, yet they are. Somehow, I feel like it's all my fault. Like I'm the one who can't handle it, while I don't think I've done anything wrong."

"You haven't done anything wrong, but neither have I." Liz took a step back. "It's too late for this. We've already had this conversation once earlier today. I don't think I can have it twice."

"Neither can I. There's nothing new to say, anyway." Jessica felt herself deflate. It had been a long day. In fact, she hadn't been able to relax fully since last night before 7 p.m.

"Maybe there is." Liz pulled her leather jacket a little tighter around her shoulders. "Maybe we should end this now. Before it gets even more painful."

"What? No," Jessica blurted out. "I don't want to end things. I'm just asking for a bit more time."

"Take all the time you need and while you do, don't invite me over if you don't want to see me. Don't take me to dinner with your friends if you're not having a good time because you're too embarrassed about what I do. It's humiliating for me. I hope you can see that."

"Won't you come in? Let's have that chat, anyway." Panic gripped like a cold fist around Jessica's heart.

"I can't give you an ultimatum, Jess. That wouldn't be fair. But I simply cannot be with someone who doesn't really want to be with me."

"But I do want to be with you. How can you even think that I don't?"

"Part of you does, yes. I do believe that. But what do you want? For us to hide inside your house forever? For me to be your stealthy lover? This was dinner with Katherine and Caitlin. You won't find anyone more open-minded than those two. And already you couldn't deal. What are you going to say when someone at work asks what your new girl-friend does for a living?"

"I'm certainly not going to tell them she's a hooker," Jessica blurted out.

"Exactly," Liz said. "That's what I thought."

"What? You want me to tell people what you do? That's just ridiculous? Like it's something to be proud of."

Jessica watched Liz lose composure in front of her eyes. Her knees seemed to buckle a little and her shoulders slumped.

"I'd best be going now." Liz turned around.

"Wait, Liz, please." Jessica rushed to her side. "Let's get you a cab first. Stay until it gets here." Jessica reached for her purse. She didn't dare touch Liz. She knew she'd gone too far.

"I'll wait outside. It shouldn't be a problem to get one." There was a trembling undertone to Liz's voice.

Jessica leapt to the door and stood in front of it. "I'm sorry. I shouldn't have said that."

"That's right." Liz straightened her spine a little. "I'm a human being. Just like you, Jess. Why can't you see that?"

"I *can*. Liz, please. I don't want to lose you. We only just met," Jessica pleaded.

Liz shook her head. "I'm willing to be understanding and I'm willing to have all the conversations you need to under-stand me and what I do and the reasons why I do it, but I draw the line at the obvious mortification you feel because of being with me." She sighed. "This is supposed to be the fun time, Jess. You can't even bear to touch me. It's obvious we're not right for each other."

"We can't just end things in the middle of the night in my hallway. We need to discuss this in the daylight, after a good night's sleep."

"I don't." Liz stepped closer to the door and grabbed the handle. "Please move, Jess. I want to leave."

"But—" Jessica had no more arguments. Everything she could say now would be a repeat of what she'd already said, and she'd said all the wrong things.

Liz might also very well be right. Jessica couldn't do this. They were too different and wanted different things. But if that was the case, why wasn't Jessica being flooded with relief because she was off the hook? Why did it feel like someone was punching her repeatedly in the gut instead?

Jessica moved away from the door. What else could she do? As torn and empty as she felt at the depressing prospect of never seeing Liz again, she'd done all the begging she could do. And she couldn't in good faith ask Liz again to stay and say they'd work it all out.

Liz opened the door and before she left, she turned around to look at Jessica. "You know, when we were talking about double standards at dinner earlier, I really hoped some message was getting across to you. Clearly, it didn't." She paused. "Bye, Jess," Liz said, and the sadness in her voice felt like the most painful punch to Jessica's gut yet.

Jessica stared at the closed door for a while longer. When a tear showed up in the corner of her eye, she quickly brushed it away. She didn't deserve to cry over this. She deserved the pain, but not the relief of tears.

Chapter Twenty-Three

JESSICA HAD BARELY SLEPT. She hadn't wanted to call Katherine in the middle of the night, but she had counted the hours until she could. It was only eight on a Sunday morning, but Jessica had to talk to someone. She'd been cooped up in her house in silence for far too long. Her heart might explode out of her chest with pent-up regret if she didn't talk to someone soon.

She dialed Katherine's number and tapped her finger on the kitchen counter while it rang. Katherine didn't pick up. Jessica could hardly blame her. Her phone was probably on silent. She had wondered if she and Liz were ever allowed to put their phone on silent—if even on Sunday mornings they should be reachable for the agency. Clearly not.

Or maybe Katherine was screening her calls. Maybe she'd been woken by the phone, had seen it was only Jessica calling, and had rolled over in bed.

Jessica made a cup of extra strong espresso and took it into the living room. She'd barely sat down when her phone rang. For a split second, she hoped it was Liz. She could have changed her mind overnight and wanted to spend Sunday together.

"Hey, Jess," Katherine sounded very chirpy for a Sunday morning. "Sorry I didn't pick up. I was in the shower."

"You're up early," Jessica said.

"So are you," Katherine replied. "It's my turn to host brunch. You know how hard the gays are to impress."

Jessica had heard about Katherine's brunches, but she'd never attended one. She didn't know that many gay men, to be honest. "I guess," she said.

"What's going on? Why are you calling me so early?"

Jessica sighed. "I wanted to ask if you were free for breakfast, but you're not, so let's get together some other time."

"There are so many red flags in what you just said. I don't even know where to start."

"Liz and I broke up. Last night after we got back from dinner. I was being a right ass. I could use one of your pep talks."

"Come to brunch," Katherine said without hesitation. "It'll take your mind off things at the very least."

"I'm not sure I'm in the mood for that."

"Of course you're not in the mood, but it beats moping at home. Come a little early, we can have a chat while you help me scramble the eggs." This made Jessica think of the eggs Liz had tried to scramble for her only a few days ago, when everything still seemed so full of hope.

"Okay, I'll happily join you." She paused. "Liz isn't going to be there, is she?"

"No," Katherine says. "Just you, me, and five fabulous gays."

———

"Basically what you're saying is that you can't be with Liz," Katherine stated matter-of-factly. Jessica wasn't being much help preparing brunch, but she had stopped by a bakery and bought a dozen fresh rolls and a pavlova for dessert.

"That's not really what I said."

"Maybe not in so many words, but I can read between the lines, Jess." Katherine stopped what she was doing and turned to Jessica, her hands on her sides. "Tell me honestly. Have you ever had a problem with our friendship?"

"What? No. You know that."

"What if I don't believe you?" There was a sudden edge to Katherine's voice.

"Come on, Kat. I've known you for many years," Jessica replied sharply. "There's a big difference between being friends with someone and dating them."

"You have to understand that Liz and I can't be apologetic about what we do. Certainly not with potential love interests. That would put us in a position of weakness and well, let's be honest, life's already no fairytale for the likes of us. We get judged all the time. By our clients. By our friends, even the ones who know us well, because of preconceived notions. By our family, if we ever find the courage to tell them. By everyone who even gets an inkling of what we do. I think it's normal Liz reacted the way she did, although I do think she could have been a bit more understanding about your feelings. It's a tricky one."

"I don't blame her for how she reacted at all. I think I might have been channeling my father last night. Or I was subconsciously, and very much prematurely, dreading his possible reaction. Long before I would even think about taking Liz home. But my mind can't help going there."

"I asked you to really think about being with Liz. It's not easy. Not everyone can do it. In fact, I dare say most people can't deal with it. There's no shame in being one of those people."

Jessica shook her head. "But I don't want to be one of those people."

"Maybe you don't get to choose." Kat cocked her head. "You're Edward Porter's daughter, after all."

"Ouch." Jessica blew out some air.

"The truth hurts." Katherine apparently really meant what she'd just said.

"You think I'm someone who can't be with a woman who's a sex worker?"

"I think there's a definite possibility of that being the case."

"But what does it take? If you got the opportunity to dream up the ideal partner for yourself, what would you want them to be like?"

Katherine chuckled. "Jesus, Jess. It's Sunday morning. Can I get back to you on that?"

Jessica chuckled with her. "Sure. First thing on Monday would be fine."

"Should I stop by your office or can I phone you?" Katherine joked.

"You make it sound so black and white, though," Jessica said. "Like I'm one and can't possibly become the other."

"If the boys weren't arriving in"—she checked her watch —"fifteen minutes, I'd remind you of the story of Katherine and Suki. But I have some trays to artfully arrange and I think you remember that story, so." Katherine turned around and got back to work.

Jessica had never known Katherine's ex Suki. She'd only heard about her. She remembered that things hadn't worked out well. Then the bell rang.

"Oh, shoot. Someone's here already." Katherine quickly rinsed her hands.

"I'll get it." Jessica painted on a smile—the one she'd used since she was a child and her mother had left—and headed for the front door.

———

The gay brunch Jessica had ended up at could not have been more different from the lesbian dinner party she had attended the night before. It seemed like not one serious word came out of these men's mouths. Jessica had been formally introduced to all five of them, and she had done her very best to remember their names, but it turned out they all addressed each other as darling or sweetie which made it impossible for her to know who was addressing whom and—even more so—who was mocking whom.

She was, however, beginning to understand why Katherine enjoyed their company so much.

"I'll sleep when I'm forty," a lanky guy with a beard—Jessica thought his name was Richard—said while he suppressed a yawn.

"You're thirty-nine, darling," someone else said.

"Oh fine." He reached for his mimosa. "I'll cut my alcohol intake in half then. I'll see. When the day comes."

"Maybe you should try cutting your Grindr time in half instead," Alan—Jessica had remembered his name—said.

Richard held a hand in front of his mouth and pretended to look upset. "What are you insinuating?"

"Yes, sweetie, what are you trying to say?" Alan's partner said. "There are plenty of boys looking for daddies on Grindr. Richard's got a lot of work ahead of him."

Katherine rolled her eyes. "You guys are so lucky. The closest thing to Grindr us poor lesbians get is the RSPCA website."

"Oh you shameless thief," Rocco, an impressively

muscled man with not a hair on his head said. "You totally stole that joke from Margaret Cho."

"I confess, but she has a point, though," Katherine said.

"There's a new lesbian at work. Well, I think she's one, at least," Chris, Rocco's equally-muscled partner, said. "I just get that feeling about her and the other day, she winked at me—you know, one of those winks of recognition—when she walked past my office. I'll try to find out if she's single for you, Kat. You never know…"

"That would be the day," Katherine said. "When one of you guys sets me up with a woman. You talk a good game, boys, but nothing, I repeat, *nothing* has ever come of it. While you and Rocco would never have met if it weren't for me."

"We owe you for that forever," Rocco said. "You'll be the best man at our wedding." He blew Kat a kiss. "But we don't hang with the lezzies that much." He looked at Jessica. "What about you, honey? Kat doesn't tickle your fancy?"

Jessica had just taken a sip from her mimosa and nearly spat out the liquid all over her plate.

"Jess and I are friends," Katherine said. "Besides, she's hurting. She needs cheering up, not being asked whether I tickle her fancy or not." Katherine winked at her.

"What's going on, sweetie?" Chris asked. "Did a mean lesbian trample all over your tender heart?"

Jessica shook her head. "Nah. I did it to myself, really."

"And here I was thinking it was all so much easier for the lesbos," Richard said. "Meet, move in, watch Netflix, happy monogamy, followed by a bout of lesbian bed death here and there, but basically domestic bliss for the rest of your lives."

"Wow," Katherine said. "You've really outdone yourself with the clichés this time, Rich. You failed to mention the U-Haul, though."

"And the macramé," Peter said.

Jessica chuckled. It was the first real laugh she'd managed since last night.

"I'll have you know," Katherine said, "that Jess and I know a lesbian couple who practice non-monogamy successfully."

"Ooh," Rocco said. "What's their secret? Do tell. I'm genuinely interested."

Katherine shrugged. "What's the secret of any relationship?" She looked at Jessica as if she held the answer. "Communication, I guess. I really wouldn't know with my track record."

"You just haven't met the right woman yet," Peter said.

"I've thought about this," Jessica said, "having been single for quite some time, and I disagree with the silly notion that there's only one person out there for everyone. I think that's bullshit. At least, in my life, among the people I know best, I haven't seen much evidence of that. Let's not forget that divorce rates are soaring."

"And that's not going to go down any time soon," Rocco said, "now that the gays are starting to get married." He apparently thought this was very funny and slapped himself on the thigh.

"I disagree with you, Jess. But maybe that's just the romantic in me," Katherine said.

"Well, maybe if you'd asked me yesterday, I would have had a different opinion." As they did every other minute, Jessica's thoughts drifted to Liz again. What was she doing right now? If things had gone differently last night, what would they have been doing together? *What if? What if? What if?*

"Are you going to keep us in suspense much longer," Peter said. "Or are you going to tell us what happened with you and that woman who left you so bitter you don't believe in love any longer?"

"That's putting it a bit dramatically," Jessica said. "I do believe in love. I'm just not a fan of the overly romanticized take on it. It can be bloody hard sometimes to fall in love." She sipped from her mimosa.

"We're still waiting for your story." Peter leaned back in his chair.

"Don't feel as though you have to entertain them with your heartache, Jess. They can go home and watch *Queer Eye* if they want some drama."

"Ooh girl, you've got the 'tude today," Rocco said.

"It's really just a matter of irreconcilable differences," Jessica said. "This woman and I, we're just too different."

"But you at least had a good tumble in the hay with her?" Chris asked.

"Oh yeah." Some glee had sneaked into Jessica's voice. "Quite the tumble."

"You go, girl." Chris held up his hand for a high five.

Flabbergasted, Jessica looked at it, then slapped her palm against his.

"This is not about sex." Rocco told his partner off. "Can't you see Jessica's in distress about this."

"At least she got something out of it," Chris said.

"You know just as well as I do that it's different for lesbians," Rocco said.

"Oh, please," Chris said. "Here we go again." He waved off Rocco's remark. "Kat, darling, back me up here."

"But what Rocco just said is so true," Katherine said in a mock-serious tone. "I have no idea what you guys are doing in my house. I'm a lesbian and you're gay men. We have the least in common of all the possible sexual orientations." She snickered.

"Kat's not a representative lesbian," Rocco said. "She has more sex than the five of us combined." He turned to the other men. "No offense, darlings."

"Let's not go overboard," Katherine said. "For that to be even remotely true, I'd need to be having sex multiple times every single day."

Richard brought a hand to his mouth. "Do you mean to say that you don't? You've just shattered my entire image of you."

Katherine shook her head. "I'm way too exclusive for that."

Jessica couldn't believe what she was hearing. These were not the conversations about sex she was used to. In fact, she wasn't used to many conversations about sex at all. But these men and Katherine talked about it as if it was just any other hobby or pastime.

Chris held up his hand to high five Katherine this time. Jessica took another sip from her mimosa and looked them all over. They all looked happy enough, chattering away on a Sunday morning. Being themselves didn't allow room for being ashamed and their self-respect clearly didn't depend on what anyone else thought of them.

As the day progressed, Jessica's admiration for them grew, and by the time she left Katherine's house, she felt as though the uptightness she'd been accused of earlier had vastly diminished just by being in the company of people who could be just as judgmental as herself when it came to superficial things, but who had learned to be free of judgment where it really mattered.

Chapter Twenty-Four

"NICOLAS IS COMING to see you at ten," Jennifer said. "And your father called. He asked that you call him back as soon as possible."

"Why did he call the office?" Jessica asked, although she could hardly expect Jennifer to have the answer to the question.

"I'm not sure." Jennifer took a step closer to Jessica's desk. "Can I get you anything? A strong coffee, perhaps? If you don't mind me saying so, you look a little pale."

"I didn't sleep well," Jessica said. "But I'll be fine. I'll gladly have that coffee, though." She gazed into Jennifer's worried face. "Is there anything else I should know?" What she really wanted to ask was: do you really need me here?

When she'd walked into the building half an hour earlier, she'd been flooded with even more dread than the week before at the prospect of working there for the foreseeable future.

Jessica had spent the better part of Sunday afternoon watching television, and it had been an excellent distraction—and perfect background noise for sleeping off her post-brunch buzz. But watching TV and working in TV were two very different things. And she couldn't stop thinking about a certain person who didn't even own a television set.

"No," Jennifer said. "I'll bring you a strong cup of coffee straight away."

Jessica sank into her chair. She didn't feel like calling her father. He'd want to ask how her weekend went. And these days, when he asked this particular question, he actually listened to the answer. He sometimes even asked a follow-up question.

Jessica could easily lie to him, but she didn't want to. Just over a week ago, she'd met Liz. The previous Monday, exactly one week ago, she'd booked her services again. As a direct consequence, Jessica had come to life again. Liz had done that. It had all happened so quickly. It might as well not have happened. Maybe she could shake off Liz's passage in her life as some crazy fever dream. Attribute it to late-stage complications after surgery.

Jessica scoffed. Was she really so afraid that she would be willing to ignore the best thing that had happened to her in years?

A knock came on the door and Jennifer brought in her coffee.

"Thanks. You're a life saver," Jessica said. She took a sip and was grateful she had made at least one meaningful contribution to the Programming Department during her short time heading it: procuring a state-of-the-art coffee machine for the break room.

Instead of calling her father, Jessica dialed Caitlin's extension. She hoped she had arrived at the office already.

"Morning, Boss," Caitlin said. "I rushed down as soon as you called. What's the Monday morning emergency?"

"Please close the door."

"Ooh, sounds ominous," Caitlin joked.

Jessica checked her watch. She had a bit of time before her meeting with Nicolas Morton.

Caitlin sat down. "Who would you like me to invite on my show? Grannie Kramer?" She sat there beaming a wide smile.

"This isn't about work."

Caitlin pursed her lips together. "I figured as much."

"Liz and I have… well, I'd say broken up but we weren't really ever together, were we?"

"I did pick up on some tension between you. The way I understood it from you, Katherine might have been a problem at the dinner, but, er, it turned out to be someone else."

"I'm sorry for behaving the way I did. It was pathetic, really. It ruined a perfectly good night."

Caitlin shrugged. "We all have bad nights. Don't worry about it."

Jessica chuckled. "Are you letting me off the hook so easily because I had cancer? It's not a free-for-all insult-who-you-want card, you know."

"I'm your friend, Jess. I'm simply not half or even a quarter as hard on you as you are on yourself. Give yourself a break." Caitlin linked her hands behind her neck and rested her head back. "My life became so much easier when I started forgiving myself for everything. It's the only way."

"You're Caitlin James," Jessica said, and remembered how Liz had fawned over her at dinner last Saturday—before it all went south. "What could you possibly have to forgive yourself for?"

Caitlin shook her head. "Every single person on this

planet has plenty of things to forgive themselves for. It can be small things or huge things. But some people prefer to hang on to their mistakes and their pain and be all victim-y about it."

"Do you mean me?" Jessica asked.

Caitlin sat up. "You've been through a rough time, Jess. It was never going to be easy to pick yourself back up, but you're doing it. So you said some things to Liz, or you made her feel bad and as though things between you couldn't work… so what? Right this minute, millions of people are making similar mistakes. It doesn't mean things can't work out. I'm sure Liz has had to endure far worse than what you've thrown at her. If you feel like you screwed up, get over it, and get her back."

Jessica's phone started ringing. It was Jennifer.

"Sorry," she said to Caitlin and picked up.

"I have your father on the line for you," Jennifer said.

"Oh Christ," Jessica said. She looked at Caitlin. "I'm going to have to take this."

Caitlin shot up out of her chair. "Call me later," she said, and scooted out the door.

Jessica took a deep breath and said, "Hello, Daddy."

"How's my favorite daughter?" her father said.

"I'm your only daughter," Jessica replied, as always.

"Still my favorite." Jessica knew he was in a good mood if he continued the joke—no matter how silly it was.

"How are you?" she asked.

"I'm good, as always. How are you?"

"Well," Jessica said.

"Well enough to come to the Porter gala next weekend?"

Jessica had completely forgotten about that, even though it was a yearly event and her presence was non-negotiable. She'd had other things on her mind lately. But she knew that turning up meant a lot to her father.

"Of course. I'll be there with bells on."

"Great." Her father paused. She could hear his breath in her ear while he was trying to find the words to say whatever he was going to say next. It was an odd thing. Edward Porter usually wasn't one to beat about the bush. His only child getting cancer had changed more about him than Jessica allowed herself to consider. But when she was faced with it like this, it was hard to ignore.

"Yes?" she asked.

"It's just that, um, an acquaintance of Christine has seen you with someone and, I guess, we were both wondering if you'd be coming to the gala alone or bringing a plus one?"

"Seen me with someone?" Jessica's heart started racing.

"Walking down the street, apparently. That's what I've been told."

Jessica relaxed. "People walk down the street with other people all the time, Daddy."

"Well, yes, of course. Sure they do. But this person who spotted you apparently told Christine that you looked as though you were very close."

"Erm, excuse me, but is this Edward Porter on the other end of the line or an impersonator pulling a prank on me?"

"You know what your stepmother's like," her father said. "She wouldn't let me off the hook until I asked you."

"Ah, good to know Christine still wears the trousers at home."

"What should I tell her?"

"The truth. That I was walking down the street with a friend. Getting some air during my convalescence. Doctor's orders and all that."

"And you'll be coming to the gala alone?" her father asked.

"Yes. Alone," Jessica confirmed, but not without a pang

of regret shooting through her. This was the same gala where, four years ago, she'd met Katherine.

"She was just a friend then?" Her father took her by surprise with that question.

"Yes, Daddy. Just a friend." Right now, Liz wasn't even her friend. In fact, Liz had never been her friend. Jessica had fallen hard and fast for her, but friendship had nothing to do with it.

"Okay," he said. "Don't work too hard."

Jessica shook her head, well aware her father couldn't see her response to more evidence of his changed behavior.

"The same goes for you," she said.

"Do you know what?" her father said. "I might actually take your advice."

———

On Tuesday afternoon Jessica found herself at home, not knowing what to do with herself. She logged onto The Lesbian Experience website and surfed to Liz's profile. In the picture that came with it, her face was obscured to protect her privacy, but her lingerie-clad body was on full display. Jessica remembered the picture hanging above Liz's bed. Then she remembered Liz's actual body all over hers. Liz's finger tracing her scar. Liz's lips on her nipple.

She read through Liz's profile again. It was all fairly vague but pretty accurate at the same time.

Liz likes to go to the gym and keep fit. Liz likes to visit art galleries and go to the opera. She has a fair complexion and short black hair.

That information wasn't too up-to-date. *Liz has bangs that fall into her eyes all the time,* Jessica corrected the profile in her head. *And she tucks it behind her ears with the cutest gesture you'll ever see.*

Jessica scrolled down and stopped at the section titled *Specialties*.

First time lesbian experiences. Liz will make you feel totally at ease. Her warmth will disarm you and she will create that special kind of atmosphere in which you can fully relax and discover what you really like.

Liz would be perfect for that. In her head, Jessica added another special skill: helping cancer survivors accept their changed bodies. She figured that wouldn't do well on the agency's website.

She scrolled down to the next section: *Most beautiful feature*: *bedroom eyes*.

Goodness, Liz's eyes.

Jessica closed the website. She didn't want to read about Liz's features on the internet. She wanted to see them in real life. Caitlin's words rang in her head. *Get over it and get her back.*

Jessica wished it were that simple. Yes, she had been insensitive and prejudiced and judgmental, but not without good reason.

In the end, it all boiled down to the choice she had to make. She got up from the couch and looked out the window. Someone had seen her walking around the streets of Pott's Point with Liz on her arm. Jessica had no idea who and she had no intention of asking her stepmother.

She put on her jacket and went for a walk—on her own. She walked all the way to the Pink Bean, retracing the route she and Liz had taken only last week.

She ordered a coffee and sat by the window, gazing out, watching the people going by. Foot traffic was high and every single time she caught the profile of a tall woman with dark hair, her heart skipped a beat.

But what would Liz be doing in this neighborhood, anyway? Come to think of it, she could have a client in

Darlinghurst. She may need a cup of coffee after and hop into that coffee shop she discovered the previous week.

Jessica shook her head. Had she really fought her way out of depression and beat cancer to feel like this? To glance at strangers in the street and hope they would be the woman who had made her feel the most alive in years? Was it really a case of love versus virtue? Because Jessica wasn't all that interested in virtue anymore.

"Hi, Jessica," a voice came from behind her. "So good to see you."

Jessica looked up and saw Sheryl standing by the table.

"How are you?" Sheryl asked.

Jessica didn't know what to say. Politeness required her to answer that she was doing fine, and physically she *was* doing well, but emotionally, she was about to fall apart.

"Can I sit?" Sheryl asked when Jessica didn't reply.

"Of course. And I'm fine, by the way." Jessica tried a smile.

"Are you?" Sheryl glanced at her with the most piercing gaze.

"Yep."

"Not back at work yet?" Sheryl asked.

"Only half days for now."

"Ah, so you're a lady of leisure in the afternoon." Sheryl narrowed her eyes and examined Jessica's face. She was about to say something—or ask a question Jessica was pretty sure she wouldn't want to answer—when Kristin showed up at their table. She put her hand on Sheryl's shoulder. It was a simple gesture, but it held so much meaning. It reminded Jessica of what she'd said at Katherine's brunch the day before. The harsh words she had spoken about love. Yet, right in front of her nose, she was presented with the very image of love. Two women who had been together for decades. Two women to whom the simple gesture of laying a hand on each other's shoulder meant very little and so much at the same time.

Jessica had turned forty-five and she'd never been the recipient of such a tiny gesture. She had, however, very much been on the receiving end of a very grand gesture. Liz's kindness, which not only shone in her eyes every time she looked at Jessica, but had been so blatantly on display when she'd coaxed Jessica to look at herself in the mirror.

"It's lovely to see you both," Jessica said. Neither Sheryl nor Kristin would ever know how truly she meant it. "But I have somewhere to be." She pushed herself out of her chair, shot the two women a smile, and went on her way.

Chapter Twenty-Five

JESSICA LOOKED out of the window of her car and gazed at the entrance of Liz's building. She'd rung the bell earlier, but nobody had answered. Either Liz wasn't home or she was ignoring her.

On the drive over to Bondi, Jessica had considered turning around quite a few times, but something had kept her foot firmly on the gas pedal and had kept her hands from turning the steering wheel. She knew exactly what that something was. The feeling Liz had given her. Jessica missed it. She missed it when she got up in the morning and faced herself in the mirror. When she glanced at her face as well as her scar. She could so easily go back to ignoring the flatness of her chest where her right breast used to be. All she had to do was turn away from the mirror or raise her glance upward a bit. But she didn't want to go back to that space where she'd lingered before she'd met Liz.

She, very simply, wanted Liz back. The alternative was feeling like she'd missed out on one of the greatest opportunities of her life, and Jessica couldn't live with that. She needed Liz to give her another chance. If only she would come home already.

Maybe she shouldn't stay in her car, ogling Liz's building like a stalker. The beach was only a few blocks away. She could go for a walk and come back later. Or she could just give Liz a call.

But Jessica found that she couldn't move. Something kept her in the car, her gaze glued to the building's entrance, waiting for the gorgeous sight of Liz to pop up in her field of vision.

———

Jessica had been sitting in her car for more than an hour, focusing on Liz's building while sipping from a bottle of water. Now she really had to use the toilet. Liz could be anywhere. She could be away for a few more hours. Maybe she had an appointment away from Sydney. An overnight in an exotic location. She had read on the agency's website that the women working there could be booked for those sort of things.

She squirmed in her seat, pressing her legs together. There was a coffee shop on the corner of the street. She could go there.

She got out of her car. It felt good to stretch her legs. She glanced around the street. She hoped Liz wouldn't arrive just then. Jessica needed to take care of her biological emergency first.

When she exited the coffee shop, a paper cup in hand, Jessica leaned against her car and scanned the street one last time. Her stake-out plan hadn't worked. She walked over to Liz's building and rang the bell one more time, on the off chance she'd arrived home while Jessica was using the facilities, but nobody answered the door.

While she drank her coffee, Jessica walked the few blocks to the beach. She threw the empty cup in a trash can and fished her phone out of her pocket. Somehow, turning up at Liz's had felt like the grand gesture she needed to make. Calling her up had seemed at the same time not enough and also harder to do. But it was her only option if she wanted to speak to Liz today. And she did.

Jessica dialed Liz's number and every time it rang, her heartbeat picked up speed. It rang seven times before it went to voicemail. Jessica listened to Liz's voicemail message. When the beep came, she found herself speechless so she hung up.

She looked at the ocean and breathed in deeply. Liz not picking up didn't necessarily mean that she didn't want to speak to her. Maybe she was driving. Or she'd just missed the call.

Or she was with a client.

Jessica forced herself to focus on the last option. Liz could very well be with a client. Say that she was, what would Jessica do if she knew this for certain? Say Liz forgave her, they made up, and Jessica was in her apartment waiting for her to come home. Could she live with that? The answer to that question was the crux of it all.

But Jessica couldn't give a hard no or yes. Imagining it wasn't the same as actually experiencing it. Besides, she had come here this afternoon because she had felt that she didn't have a choice. Liz had been placed on her path for a reason. It had hit her—like a shudder all the way into her bones— when she'd seen Sheryl and Kristin simply standing together. What was virtue worth without love? It wasn't a choice. It was just another example of Jessica being afraid to live her life to the fullest.

Chapter Twenty-Six

AFTER SHE WALKED BACK to her car, Jessica decided to give ringing Liz's bell one last try. She'd been gone for a good twenty minutes. Plenty of time for Liz to have come home— and not picked up her phone.

Jessica pressed her finger to the bell. It could very well be the last time she did so. But at least she had tried. Or maybe she would come back tomorrow. She didn't know.

The buzz of the intercom crackled, snapping Jessica out of her spiral of self-pity. "Yes?" Liz's voice said.

"Liz, hi. It's me." Didn't Liz have a video intercom system? "Jessica."

"Yes. I can see you. What do you want?"

Jessica hoped she was looking into the camera. "I would really like to speak with you. Can I come up?"

"You've sure been persistent enough," Liz said, and buzzed her in without further ado.

Jessica pushed open the door and called the elevator. What did Liz mean about her having been persistent? And what on earth was Jessica going to say to her? Would sorry be enough? She breathed deeply in and out while the elevator took her to Liz's floor. When she stood in the hallway, she found Liz's door ajar. She pushed it open and stepped inside the apartment.

Jessica didn't see Liz, so she figured she must be waiting for her inside. She closed the front door and headed into the living room.

Liz was looking out of the window, her arms crossed in front of her.

"Hi," Jessica said.

Liz didn't turn around.

"You're lucky you didn't get a parking ticket," Liz said. "I was surprised you didn't pay for your parking, I must say. It just seems like something you would always do."

"What? I'm not sure—"

"Your car's been parked across the street for two hours."

"You were home all this time?" Jessica was confused.

Still with her back to Jessica, Liz nodded.

"Why didn't you answer?"

"Why would I?" Liz finally turned around.

Jessica didn't know what to say to that. "I'm sorry." She felt it best to launch directly into an apology. "You have no reason to. I just… really wanted to see you."

"Why's that?" Liz uncrossed her arms and leaned against the window sill.

"To apologize for, um, not treating you with the respect you deserve. For putting my own insecurities above… everything else."

Liz sighed, but didn't say anything.

Jessica took a step closer. "I'm not here to give you a big declaration of love, but I am here to ask for another chance."

"What's changed?" Liz was wearing a very loose t-shirt and the sleeve had just slipped off her impressive right shoulder, baring it. "Don't tell me *you* have, because I don't think that's possible in just three days."

"Meeting you has changed me, though. I think you know that too." Jessica stopped herself from taking another step closer.

Liz shook her head. "The only thing I do know is that I don't know all that much about you. And what I do know about you, I don't care for that much."

"You can be really harsh sometimes," Jessica said.

"Likewise," Liz said. She glared at Jessica but something in her face had softened.

"I'm here, Liz," Jessica said. "I'm here because it's the only place I want to be. Nothing else is of interest to me. You made me feel things…" She shook her head. "I can't even begin to tell you."

"How do you propose I react to this?" Liz held up her hand. "Don't give me your dream scenario, just give me an honest assessment. If you were in my shoes, what would you do?"

Jessica couldn't stop a small smile from forming on her lips. "That's an impossible question and you know it."

Liz pursed her lips together. She looked at her watch ostentatiously. "What if I told you I had to meet a client in an hour. How would you react to that?"

"I would say…" Jessica racked her brain. So much seemed to depend on her reply. She looked at Liz, at how she stood there, the light from outside like a halo around her, her shoulder bare. Her eyes were challenging Jessica, but they conveyed kindness as well.

"Well," Liz said when Jessica remained silent, "what's it going to be?"

Jessica locked her gaze on Liz's. She had stopped racking her brain. The answer to Liz's question wasn't to be found in her logical mind, anyway. It had to come from her gut. "I would say," she repeated. "Care to practice on me?"

Liz burst out into a chuckle. "Oh really?" She brought her hands to her sides. "That's what you would say?"

"I just said it, didn't I?" Jessica shuffled closer.

Liz regarded her from under her eyelashes. "Very well." She sank her front teeth into her bottom lip. "Come here." She reached out her hand.

Jessica looked at it before she took hold of it. She tried to keep a calm expression on her face, but on the inside, nerves were tearing through her.

Liz gently tugged Jessica toward her. They stood inches apart. Jessica could smell Liz's perfume and the scent had the same effect on her as a kiss from Liz's lips would. Just to stand so close to her was enough to make Jessica's knees tremble.

Liz brought her hands to Jessica's waist and spun her around. She pushed Jessica's backside against the window sill and pressed her lower body against Jessica's.

"Did you mean what you just said?"

Jessica couldn't speak so she just nodded.

"I need you to say it. Do you stand by it?"

"I—I do," Jessica stammered.

"Do you give me permission to put what you just said to the test?" Liz's voice was solemn and serious.

Jessica nodded again. If this meant Liz was going to put her hands all over her, she wanted nothing more.

"Say it," Liz whispered.

Jessica swallowed and looked into Liz's eyes. "I give you permission."

"Good." Liz leaned in as though she was going to kiss Jessica, but then deviated from her path, and planted a kiss on Jessica's neck. She was going straight for Jessica's soft spot. She traced a wet path along Jessica's neck and Jessica was glad she had the window sill for support. When Liz kissed her like that, she needed all the support she could get.

Liz stopped kissing her neck abruptly. Jessica opened her eyes and gazed at her. Liz stood there with a triumphant grin on her face. She brought her hands to the hemline of her t-shirt and pulled it over her head.

"I saw you staring at my shoulder earlier," she said.

Jessica's gaze was pulled away from Liz's face to her bra-clad breasts and that impressively square shoulder line. Her clit started pulsing between her legs. If this was Liz's idea of foreplay today, she was up for it.

"Now." Liz pressed herself against Jessica again. "As we're standing in front of the window, I'm not going to take off my bra." Her smile transformed into a grin.

This made Jessica acutely aware that they were standing in front of said window. She had stared at this window for a good long while that afternoon and not once spotted Liz in her apartment. Maybe because she thought she wasn't home, but still. She had her back to the street below. She could work with this. And with the sensation of Liz's breasts pressing into her. Liz's knee spreading her legs apart. Liz's breath traveling over her skin.

Liz brought a finger to Jessica's face and traced her jawline with it. She dragged it all the way underneath her chin and let it travel upward to her cheekbone, then down past her cheek to end up dancing along her lips.

Liz's finger stopped in the middle of Jessica's bottom lip. Liz held Jessica's gaze then slowly pushed her finger inside Jessica's mouth.

Jessica sucked Liz's finger inside. She twirled her tongue around it as though it was the last thing her tongue would ever touch.

While her finger remained in Jessica's mouth, Liz leaned to her side and whispered in her ear, "Remember, this is a test." She paused. "I need to know that you want me to touch you. That you really, really want it." While she bit gently into Jessica's earlobe, she flipped open the button of her jeans with her free hand. "I'm going to need you to come for me," she whispered. "Do you think you can do that?"

Jessica's mouth was too filled with Liz's finger to speak so she just nodded. The way her clit was buzzing in her panties, she figured she wouldn't have any problem with that at all.

Liz stopped speaking. She unzipped Jessica's jeans. She stood straighter so she came face to face with Jessica again. She withdrew her finger from between Jessica's lips and slipped her hand inside Jessica's panties.

A split second later, Liz's wet finger was circling Jessica's clit.

She gasped for air at the first contact. Liz's touch was light but deft. She kept her gaze on Jessica and Jessica lost herself in Liz's bedroom eyes. There was no doubt in her mind that she would pass this test with flying colors. She wanted Liz and she would show her just how much.

Jessica wrapped her fingers around the ledge of the window sill. Liz's other hand cupped her jaw and Jessica pushed her head against it. It was the only physical contact between them. Liz's hand against her cheek, and her wet finger circling Jessica's clit. But beneath the surface, so much more was going on. Jessica was surrendering to Liz. She was saying, by means of her body's reaction, that she accepted Liz and the choices she had made in her life. The choices she'd be making in the future and the life she had chosen to live.

Liz's circling motions grew faster, as did the rhythm of Jessica's breath. She felt in perfect sync with Liz, this woman who had been so unspeakably kind to her. Who had brought her back to life. How could she even have considered not wanting to see her anymore? Especially when this burgeoning ecstasy flowing through her was a big part of what being with Liz meant.

Jessica might have hired Laurel in the past. She had always justified it to herself as an act of self-care. Something to take away the loneliness, if just for an hour or two. The joy of an orgasm shared with another woman. It seemed to be something Jessica craved. But it receded into nothingness compared to what she was experiencing now. This exquisite woman's hands on her. This was an act way beyond self-care. This was Jessica opening herself up to the possibility of love—and accepting, along with slowly coming to terms with the changes to her body, that she was worthy of it.

"Oh, Liz," she moaned. It was as though saying Liz's name sent extra bursts of delicious lightning from Liz's finger to her clit. "Liz," Jessica repeated.

She closed her eyes as warmth exploded inside of her. She let her cheek drop all the way against Liz's waiting hand. Jessica's legs shook and she gasped for more air. "Oh, Liz," she said on a sigh, and sank deeper against the window sill.

She opened her eyes and stared into Liz's eyes. That small, triumphant grin was back on her lips. Liz's hand didn't retreat. She kept it inside Jessica's panties. Liz tilted her head as though studying Jessica's face, gauging her expression for something. Had Jessica not passed the test? Either way, she'd like to sit down, or at least collapse into Liz's arms, kiss her all over—and repay the favor.

Liz's tongue flicked over her lips. Jessica felt Liz's hand stir in her panties. She wasn't retreating though. Oh no. She was parting Jessica's nether lips and then, oh so easily, she slipped inside Jessica.

"Oh," Jessica exclaimed.

"Come for me again," Liz said.

"Wh—I—" Jessica wasn't capable of actually saying words, although she did want to protest. Was this still part of the test? She wasn't sure she could do this. She'd just come at

Liz's fingertip already. What more could possibly be expected of her?

Liz thrust inside of her gently—easily. Jessica must be soaking wet.

"You can do it," Liz said, not a shimmer of doubt in her voice. "I'll make sure of that." This time, when she leaned in, she did kiss Jessica on the lips. As her finger stroked high inside of Jessica, her tongue slipped inside Jessica's mouth, and Jessica started to believe what Liz had just said.

She threw her arms around Liz's neck. Jessica knew she had passed the test already. In fact, there'd never been any test. There had been her and Liz looking at each other, knowing that something inside of them made them belong together.

Jessica had no idea what magic Liz's finger was working inside of her. She thought she'd spent all her arousal on the first orgasm, but maybe it had just made her more excited. Liz's finger was insistent and it felt like so much more of Liz was inside of her. Jessica felt Liz's arm working as she fucked her, she felt Liz's naked shoulder rub against her as her finger thrust inside her. Her tongue was soft against hers. Its touch delicate, unlike the touch inside her pussy. Liz had ramped up the rhythm another notch and, for the second time that afternoon, Jessica let go.

She was able to surrender again because it was Liz doing these things to her. Liz, who had been at the center of her world since she'd met her. As she came, Jessica knew she had reached yet another level of feeling alive, of being her true self. She would always be the Jessica Porter who had suffered from depression and cancer and acute uptightness, but she would also be Nicole Elizabeth Griffith's girl, and that changed everything.

After Liz had withdrawn her hand, she smirked at Jessica

and said, "I just wanted to reward your persistence with some of my own."

Jessica chuckled. "Let me catch my breath and I'll show you how much more I have in me." She drew Liz closer again and kissed her on the lips.

Chapter Twenty-Seven

"I'm not really meeting a client today," Liz said.

Jessica lay with her head on Liz's naked chest. "I figured as much."

"I'm meeting someone tomorrow, though," Liz said.

"Okay." Jessica pushed herself up. "But what are you doing on Saturday?"

"Hopefully not going to another disastrous dinner party with you." Liz smiled at her.

"I have an even better proposal." Jessica leaned on her elbow. "Will you come to the annual Edward Porter Charity Gala with me?"

Liz's eyes grew wide. "You want to introduce me to your family?"

"Nah, I'll save that ordeal for later. We can just show up and not talk to them."

Liz shook her head. "You're so strange sometimes."

"I guess that beats being harsh."

"I was being harsh on you, I admit that," Liz said. "But for your information, I already wanted to plunge my hand down your panties while you were still in the elevator."

"Must be because you were watching me through the window all afternoon. All that desperation on display. Must have been very arousing."

"Once you were up here, you'd already passed the test."

"So, what do you say?"

"To what? Meeting your family?" Liz asked.

"It's just my father, stepmother, and a few distant cousins. It's only called the Edward Porter Gala because of my dad's grandiosity. It's more a business networking thing than anything else."

"I thought it was for charity?"

"It is. Attending the dinner alone costs a fortune, and there's also an auction. It's especially for people who want to remain in my father's good graces."

"You make it sound like so much fun."

"I have to go. My father—well, my stepmother really, has been organizing this event for nine years straight and I've never once taken a date."

"How come?" Liz extended her hand and stroked Jessica's arm. "A woman like you?"

"For the longest time, my schedule was way too packed for something as frivolous as a date. When I did find myself with some unexpected time on my hands, I was too depressed to attract another woman."

"Is that why you hired Laurel? Because you didn't have time to find a date?"

Jessica sighed. "Among other reasons, I guess."

"What were the other reasons?" Liz kept stroking Jessica's arm.

Jessica arched up her eyebrows. She rolled onto her side to be more comfortable. "After I met Katherine and she told me what she did, I got really curious. And, well, I was a woman in my prime, yet nobody was touching me. Plus there was the sheer excitement of it all."

"So you made the call to the agency?"

Jessica nodded. "Yes, the first time I called, they asked me a bunch of questions."

"You weren't ordering pizza, after all," Liz said.

Jessica nodded. "The first time I set a date with Laurel, I cancelled an hour before she was supposed to arrive. I was too nervous. I couldn't go through with it."

"That happens all the time. The thought of hiring an escort can be very exciting, but actually meeting someone is another ballgame."

"In the end, I was too curious to let the thought go completely," Jessica continued. "I did go through with the second appointment." A smile appeared on Jessica's face at the memory. "Laurel was so nice. So natural. A lot like you. It takes something special to put people at ease like that."

Liz didn't say anything for a while. Then she looked at Jessica, her hand still on her arm. "The only reason I will ever give up this job is for me. Can you understand why I can't do it for someone else? Where that would leave me in the power dynamic of a relationship?"

"I'm trying to." Jessica put her hand over Liz's. "I can hardly sweep into your life—as a client, no less—and expect you to change everything about it for me."

"This job is my independence. In a few years, it will sponsor my dream. I'm so close, I can already imagine it. The Liz Griffith Gallery."

"My father is a big art collector as well," Jessica said. "My stepmother pretends to be, but she never had... I don't really know what it is you need in order to know what's going to be big or not."

"Knowledge. Patience. Willingness to do research. A degree in Art History helps as well."

"Christine has none of those things."

"Your father does?"

Jessica thought for a while. "Apart from the degree… yes, I think he does."

"Then I can't wait to meet him," Liz said. "But…I'm going to say something that's extremely contentious in my line of work. Something I've lost and gained dates over in equal measure." She smirked at Jessica. "I don't wear dresses." She waggled her eyebrows. "I look pretty dashing in a tux, though."

"Oh, I'm sure you do." Jessica leaned in to kiss her. She didn't want to think about Liz seeing a client tomorrow, or anyone who might recognize her at the gala. Instead she lost herself in the tender touch of Liz's lips, how her tongue slipped into her mouth, so assuredly, and focused only on this moment. She didn't yet know how else to deal with anything that might come her way, but she had dealt with plenty of things in the past. And look where she was now. Naked, in the arms of a gorgeous, intelligent, art-loving woman who, no doubt, would be the tux-wearing belle of the ball.

Chapter Twenty-Eight

In the back of the car, on the way to the gala, Jessica couldn't keep her eyes off Liz.

Liz hadn't lied. She indeed looked stunning in a tux, oozing equal portions of feminine and masculine energy at the same time. Jessica had only to glance at her and a slew of butterflies rose up in her stomach. But those butterflies were not only amorous hormones acting up. If they were only that, she would have been able to keep her knee from bouncing up and down the way it was.

Liz put her hand on Jessica's jittery leg.

"I've been to quite a few of these," Liz said. "So no need to worry about my dreadful posh events etiquette."

Jessica chuckled. "It's not you I'm worried about. It's my father. He's been so different lately." In her head, Jessica again went over the phone call she'd made to her father a few days earlier. He'd been strangely speechless when she'd told him she would, after all, be bringing someone to the gala. As though he was fighting back a tear. "I'm wondering if I should speak to his doctor."

"Why?" Liz asked. "Because his daughter's illness has

miraculously put him in touch with his emotions?" She shook her head. "It's a gift. Not something to worry about."

"It's disconcerting when you've known him your whole life."

"Maybe you should speak to his wife. See how she feels about it." Liz nudged her knee against Jessica's.

"Goodness no. Let's leave Christine out of it."

"I'm even more curious to meet them now."

Jessica sighed. "Maybe this was the wrong occasion. I should have introduced you to them privately."

"But you didn't want to go to the gala alone," Liz said matter-of-factly.

"Correct."

"And your father sounded over the moon that you're bringing me," Liz continued.

Jessica nodded.

"Well, perhaps not me specifically." Liz threw in a chuckle. "You're quite sure Christine has never hired a lesbian escort for some harmless fun on a weekday afternoon?"

Jessica slapped Liz on the thigh playfully. "Stop it." She had to suppress a giggle, though.

"I do predict I won't be the only working girl or boy at this event. People with enough money to spare, to casually spend five grand on a charity dinner, enjoy having some eye candy on their arm."

"Not even I can deny that." Jessica flashed her a smile.

The car stopped.

"We've arrived," the driver said. He got out and opened the door.

————

Jessica's father did a double-take as she and Liz approached.

Perhaps he hadn't expected his daughter to turn up alongside a woman in a tuxedo. He quickly regrouped and threw his arms wide. He hugged them both. Then looked Jessica up and down.

"You look smashing, dear," he said. "As always."

Then he grinned at Liz. "You make a stunning pair."

"Thanks, Daddy," Jessica said. She glanced at Christine, who stood next to her father, doing her very best to not look too uncomfortable. At least she was trying.

"You must come to dinner next week. No excuses," her father said and winked at them, once again reminding Jessica that he was not the same man she'd known before her surgery.

When she'd suffered from depression, he had shown his fatherly love in the way she was accustomed to: throwing money around and making sure all the bad press went away quickly.

"I would love to, Mr. Porter," Liz said. "It's a real pleasure to be here."

Jessica was pulled from her thoughts by Liz being overly formal. She looked around. While she and Liz had greeted her father and Christine, a group of people had formed around them. It was clear that most of them wanted to say hello to her father and stepmother.

"We'll talk more later," Jessica said. She pulled Liz aside.

Before she had a chance to step away, her father put a hand on Jessica's shoulder and shot her the kind of joyful smile she wasn't used to seeing on his face.

"How many marks out of ten for that?" Liz asked when they'd moved away. "For impressing your old man upon first meeting him?" She leaned in and whispered in Jessica's ear. "For your information, I can now officially confirm that your stepmother has never availed of my services."

A waiter waltzed by with a tray of champagne glasses. They each took one.

"Will you tell me when you see someone who has?" Jessica asked.

Liz painted a smile on her lips and shook her head. "No can do, and you know it."

———

"Shall I bid on this?" Jessica asked. The auction was on its last legs and she had yet to make her first bid.

"A two-night stay at The Belgrave Spa and Resort in Katoomba, all expenses paid," the auctioneer repeated. "After you've paid for them in advance, of course." He paused. "Can I start the bidding at three thousand dollars? Any takers?"

Seven people raised their hands.

Jessica looked at Liz. "Do you want to go on a weekend getaway with me?"

"I most definitely do."

Jessica joined the bidding. The price quickly went up to six thousand dollars, until it was just her and one last tenacious bidder left.

She craned her neck to check out her competition. "Who is that woman?" she said under her breath, not expecting an answer.

"A tough cookie with very deep pockets," Liz said. "You may want to brace yourself for a real bidding war."

Jessica's eyes grew wide. "You know her?"

Liz nodded.

"Do we have six and a half?" the auctioneer said.

The woman raised her hand. Jessica quickly followed suit.

"You may also want to set yourself a top price you don't want to go over before this gets out of hand," Liz said.

Jessica shook her head. "No bloody way. My pockets are equally deep. I'll show her."

"Jess, I'll take you on a weekend to Katoomba. It's not worth this kind of money nor… competition," Liz said.

"It is to me." Jessica kept raising her hand.

"The Belgrave sure is popular," the auctioneer joked. "But let's remind ourselves that all proceeds of this auction go to Sydney Children's Hospital," he said. "Do we have a bid of ten thousand dollars?"

The woman raised her hand.

Liz put her hand on Jessica's knee. "Let it go." She raised her eyebrows.

"Going once," the auctioneer said.

Jessica looked at Liz. What point was she trying to prove, anyway? That she had more money than this woman she believed had hired Liz's services? What could that possibly accomplish?

The auctioneer looked straight at her. "Twice." He tilted his head.

Jessica glanced in the direction of the woman who was about to outbid her. She was staring straight ahead of her, as though she had no eye for anyone else.

Liz squeezed her knee and whispered, "Just let it go."

"Sold," the auctioneer said. "The two-day getaway in Katoomba is going to Mrs. Robinson. Congratulations. Thank you on behalf of Sydney Children's Hospital and enjoy."

"I was just driving up the price," Jessica said. "Doing my bit for charity."

"You could just make a donation if it's that important to you," Liz said.

Jessica examined Liz's face. She had to know. She leaned

toward Liz and asked, "Is that Mrs. Robinson a client of yours? Is that why she was being so tenacious?"

"Don't ask me that," Liz replied, and by saying nothing she had just said everything.

"She's probably jealous because I'm here with you," Jessica continued.

"Jess, I'm serious," Liz said. "You really have to let this go. Okay?" Her voice was firm.

Jessica nodded, but she couldn't help throwing another glance at Mrs. Robinson. Jessica guessed she was in her early fifties. She'd need to ask her father what he knew about her.

Or, as Liz had suggested, she could just let it go.

They sat through another few bidding wars, none of which Jessica felt inclined to participate in, until the auction ended and the dancing started.

People got up from their seats and either danced or milled about to start conversations with acquaintances. Jessica's father was in his element and she was glad he had this evening. She was, for the first time in a long while, happy for him.

Just as Liz had convinced Jessica to have a dance with her, and they were about to get up, Mrs. Robinson appeared next to their table.

Jessica was too flabbergasted to say anything.

"Congratulations," Liz said, and extended her hand. "You drive a hard bargain."

Mrs. Robinson took Liz's hand in hers and held it for far too long according to the etiquette Jessica was raised with.

"You're Edward's daughter, aren't you?" she asked Jessica. She finally let go of Liz's hand but didn't offer to shake Jessica's. Mrs. Robinson probably believed Jessica had hired Liz for the night, as her plus one.

"Yes." Jessica kept her tone clipped. She didn't have it in

her to be friendly to this woman. "Enjoy your stay in Katoomba. It's beautiful there this time of year."

"Oh, I know, dear." She painted a wicked smile on her lips. "And I'm not the only one." She shot Liz a quick wink and turned on her heels.

"Bloody hell," Jessica said. "What was that?"

Liz came to stand in front of her and put her hands on Jessica's shoulders. "Let's dance," she said.

"I'm not sure I know how to let this go," Jessica said.

"It's very simple," Liz said and kissed her on the cheek. "Dance with me."

"Dance with you?" Jessica arched up her eyebrows. "And that's going to solve everything?"

"It won't, but it will at least take your mind off things. Turn some heads. Make you feel some joy in here." She touched her chest.

Jessica nodded and allowed Liz to lead her to the dance floor. *This is the real test*, she thought. There might be many more to come.

Then she looked at Liz who stood there waiting in her impeccable tux and with her warm, inviting smile, hand outstretched. There was no way Liz would ever look at the likes of Mrs. Robinson like that. This particular intensity in her glance was reserved solely for the woman Liz was obviously falling in love with.

For Jessica.

Jessica stepped into Liz's embrace and Liz's warm strength seeped into her as they slow-danced to an old song. Jessica didn't remember the song title, but it must have been requested by her father because she remembered him playing it at home when she was younger.

"You understand me," the lyrics went. "You're you and that's why I love you."

Liz pulled her closer and Jessica melted into her embrace.

She pushed the thought of Mrs. Robinson from her mind and concluded that if she wanted to pass the test, all she had to do was let go. Life was what it was. It certainly wasn't a fairytale. Yet here Jessica was, dancing with her fairytale princess in a tuxedo.

Epilogue

"Darling." Jessica's father pulled her into a tight hug. "Congratulations."

Liz stood next to her and she was next in line for a Daddy Porter hug. Jessica hadn't told her father what Liz did for a living. She and Liz had discussed it, but when it came down to it, it wasn't any of his business. And this art gallery they'd opened together provided Liz with the perfect cover.

"Elizabeth," Jessica's father said, and threw his arms wide for Liz.

Jessica watched their embrace with a combination of delight and wonder. At least her father had shown some of his old personality when Jessica had told him she was quitting her job at ANBC. She had given him a few days to compose himself after delivering the news—a few days he had sorely needed. But compose himself, he had.

"Don't let anyone else buy anything before I do," Jessica's father said. "I want to make the first official purchase."

"You'd best start browsing straight away then," Liz said.

"I'll need you to give me a tour," Jessica's father said.

"Come on then." Liz winked at Jessica and took her father by the arm.

Jessica watched them walk toward a painting together and wondered how her father would react if he found out that Liz worked for an escort agency. It was not unthinkable that he already knew. He could have had someone do a background check on Liz. But even if he knew, he hadn't said anything. And he and Liz seemed to get on like a house on fire.

"Jess, hello." Jessica was snapped out of her reverie by more guests arriving. It was Katherine and her gaggle of gays. Kisses and congratulations were exchanged, glasses of champagne distributed.

When most of the invitees had arrived, Katherine and Jessica stood chatting in a corner of the gallery, overlooking the crowd.

"It's a real problem in our industry," Katherine said.

"What is?" Jessica asked.

"Clients falling in love with escorts." She looked at Jessica. "It comes with the territory of offering a lesbian experience, I guess."

"Says the woman who gave me such a hard time about having feelings for the woman I'd hired."

"I did so with good reason, Jess. Clients fall for us all the time. Things can get really tricky if it's not mutual."

Jessica chuckled. "So when you made that joke about the RSPCA being the closest thing to Grindr for lesbians, you actually meant to say escort agencies."

"The RSPCA is cheaper though."

"And you get a pet *and* a girlfriend at the same time."

"Double whammy," Katherine said.

"Remember when I asked you if a client had ever fallen for you?" Jessica found her friend's glance.

Katherine nodded.

"How about the other way around? Have you ever fallen for a client?"

"What's with all the questions? Don't you have some guests to entertain?" Katherine smiled good-naturedly.

"Just curious, as it seems to be quite a common occurrence."

Katherine shook her head. "I haven't. I guess I'm more the kind of girl who looks for romance in other places."

"How about art gallery openings?" Jessica asked.

"Sure," Katherine said. They both let their gaze wander over the crowd. "Meanwhile, I'll just keep on having my fun."

"What's your retirement dream?" Jessica asked. "Liz wanted to open an art gallery. Do you have something you're saving for?"

"I might have," Katherine said.

Jessica turned to her. "How long have I known you?" She put her hands on her hips. "You've never told me about your dream?"

"You never asked."

"It never really occurred to me," Jessica said. "Don't keep me in suspense. What is it?"

"A coffee shop," Katherine said. "Rocco and I have been talking about it for years. He believes in the black gold as much as I do. When I retire, that's what I would like to do. Start our very own coffee shop."

"Well then, please allow me to introduce you to two people who know all about coffee shops." Jessica took Katherine by the hand and led her to where Kristin and Sheryl were standing.

———

"Your father bought two works," Liz said.

Jessica rolled her eyes, even though she was grateful.

"He really doesn't come across as the man you described to me when we first met."

"That's because he's a different man. It only took me losing a breast to change him into a human being." Jessica curved her arm around Liz's waist. "What do you think? Successful opening?"

"Spectacular," Liz said. "Art is big business and your father's crowd knows it." She smiled at Jessica. "I'm so glad we've been able to put your privilege to good use."

Jessica snickered. "No more poor little rich girl for me. I'm owning it."

Liz pressed her side against Jessica's. "I'm really happy," she said. "This is just… perfect."

They overlooked the gallery, which was empty apart from a few people from the catering company cleaning up.

"I'm happy too," Jessica said.

"I bet I can make you a tiny bit happier," Liz said. "There's something in my back pocket for you."

A tingle rushed up Jessica's spine. "For me?" She turned Liz around. She felt inside and found a small envelope.

"Open it," Liz said.

Jessica tore at the flap, which was glued shut too tightly for her liking. When she managed to open it, she pulled out a card that said: The Belgrave Spa and Resort in Katoomba is delighted to invite you for a two-night stay.

A smile appeared on Jessica's face.

"And guess what?" Liz folded her arms around Jessica's neck. "It didn't cost me ten grand."

"Let's hope Mrs. Robinson isn't there at the same time," Jessica said. "I don't want you working when we're there."

Liz chuckled. "I never confirmed that so you can keep your assumptions to yourself."

"How about when you retire. Will you be able to confirm some things to me then?"

"Nope. Some things I'll have to take to my grave. Like how we met."

"What are you talking about? We met at an art gallery. An artist we both like had a show. It was love at first sight. It made us want to start an art gallery together not long after. And here we are, six months later."

"Keep telling yourself that," Liz said. "But I'll always know the truth."

"So will I," Jessica said. "The escort agency screwed up and there you were."

"The perfect story for any dinner party." Liz grinned.

"Yep." Jessica nodded. "We can easily shock people with that for the rest of our lives."

Liz leaned in and kissed her on the lips. "How about you take me home now? I'm not used to the kind of job where I have to be on my feet for so long."

Jessica shook her head and suppressed a giggle. "Come on then." She took Liz by the hand. "I'll have you on your back in no time."

Acknowledgments

Dear Reader,

I hope you enjoyed reading Jessica's story. I sure had a ball writing it, mainly because, just like Jess, I had a massive crush on Liz. It's not Liz I want to talk about in this note, however… because, well, I usually talk about myself, don't I?

How does this book possibly pertain to Harper, you might think. Well, let me lay it all bare for you again. (Just my emotional exhibitionist streak rearing its head again!) I've been one of those fortunate people who've never had to deal with a cancer scare (although, just like about everyone, I've seen it touch many lives around me.) What I have experienced, however, is what it feels like to wake up from general anesthetic with only one breast intact.

A few years ago I had breast reduction surgery and a few things didn't go according to plan. I ended up needing a second surgery, which reduced one of my breasts to a lower cup-size, and took away most of my nipple. Not a mastectomy by a long shot, but it took me almost a year before I could look at my chest in the mirror again.

In previous author notes, it has been well established that I'm of the hypersensitive, rather squeamish type. A characteristic I was able to put to good use when channeling Jessica's fears. When you wake up one day and your body is not how it once was, it takes some getting used to. But I got used to it (I even got over my doctor putting actual leeches on my nipple to 'stimulate blood flow' before deciding to operate again -- real life *Game of Thrones* really isn't as fun as watching it on TV!)

I didn't have Liz to pull me through the bad times, but I did have my wonderful wife, Caroline, who put her half-British stiff-upper-lip-ness aside and assured me that to her, I was and always would be the same person I was when my two breasts were still intact.

My editor, Cheyenne Blue, knows more about me than most, that's how good a friend she is. (She squirmed when I told her about the leeches, though.) I also couldn't wish for a better person to entrust my scandalous manuscripts to.

My super-sweet beta-reader Carrie claims I'm corrupting her (and I'm proud to do so), nevertheless, her enthusiasm is always a bright moment during the nerve-racking process of putting out a book.

I've been putting my beloved Launch Team to the test, not only with the number of books I ask them to read and review, but also with the subjects I throw at them. But they always handle everything with grace and kindness.

Last but not least, Dear Reader, I must admit that I sometimes underestimate you, and think my themes are too salacious or contentious for you, after which you don't hesitate to tell me that they're decidedly not, and who's the prude now? Point very much taken. Thank you for sticking with me all this time. For one, I would never be able to expose myself so emotionally if it weren't for you reading all my words.

Thank you.

About the Author

Harper Bliss is the author of the *Pink Bean* series, the *High Rise* series, the *French Kissing* serial and many other lesbian romance titles. She is the co-founder of Ladylit Publishing and My LesFic weekly newsletter.

Harper loves hearing from readers and you can get in touch with her here:

www.harperbliss.com
harperbliss@gmail.com

Printed in Poland
by Amazon Fulfillment
Poland Sp. z o.o., Wrocław

53861717R00134